"Wha

There, th
sounded
time he could get away with *not* being in this
woman's presence.

"Before we sign in..."

"Yes?" He looked up from the book, already sensing
he wasn't going to like whatever Bella planned to
say.

"Are the cabins— I don't really know how to ask this,
so I'm just going to ask."

Of course you are.

"Are the cabins cleaned on a regular basis?"

"Yes, they are. Why do you ask?"

"They just look a little...unkempt, at least from the
outside. A fresh coat of paint would really spruce
things up," she added helpfully.

His eyes took in the woman and drew an immediate
conclusion: 100 percent city. He knew the type. But
these were guests, he reminded himself, and the
ranch needed guests.

Even ones that had already caused his insides to do
a dance filled with missteps.

Donna Gartshore loves reading and writing. She also writes short stories, poetry and devotionals. She often veers off to the book section in the grocery store when she should be buying food. Besides talking about books and writing, Donna loves spending time with her daughter, Sunday family suppers and engaging online with the writing community.

Books by Donna Gartshore

Love Inspired

Instant Family
Instant Father
Finding Her Voice
Finding Their Christmas Home
A Secret Between Them
The Courage to Love
The Rancher's Prayer

Visit the Author Profile page at LoveInspired.com.

THE RANCHER'S PRAYER

DONNA GARTSHORE

LOVE INSPIRED
INSPIRATIONAL ROMANCE

LOVE INSPIRED®
INSPIRATIONAL ROMANCE

ISBN-13: 978-1-335-62110-8

The Rancher's Prayer

Copyright © 2025 by Donna Lynn Gartshore

Recycling programs
for this product may
not exist in your area.

Love Inspired
22 Adelaide St. West, 41st Floor
Toronto, Ontario M5H 4E3, Canada
www.LoveInspired.com

Printed in Lithuania

MIX
Paper | Supporting
responsible forestry
FSC® C021394

To appoint unto them that mourn in Zion, to give unto them beauty for ashes, the oil of joy for mourning, the garment of praise for the spirit of heaviness; that they might be called trees of righteousness, the planting of the Lord, that he might be glorified.
—*Isaiah* 61:3

This one is especially for my mother, Diane Bickle, who is one of the strongest, most determined and giving people I know. She has taught me that you don't have to be a fighter to be strong.

As always, thanks to my daughter and sisters for your ongoing support.

I couldn't write these stories without the grace of our Lord. For everything He gives me, I am filled with gratitude.

Chapter One

When the Saskatchewan prairie sky exploded with the burnt orange and glowing pinks of the setting sun just as the sign that said New Hope Ranch came into view, Arabella—"please call me Bella"—Lark chose to take it as a sign that she had made the right decision to spend summer at the therapy horse ranch with her twelve-year-old daughter, Lily.

Not that she really believed in signs. She did believe in God and in what the Bible said about Him. But, even with that, the practical side of her told her that you ended up where you wanted to be by having a plan and working hard.

But after the way the last couple of weeks had gone, weeks that made her understand why people didn't want to claim that things couldn't get worse, she was ready for all the reassurance she could get.

She stole a quick glance at Lily, who was sleeping, her small mouth slightly open and emitting a soft snore.

Sometimes when a shadow happened to hit Lily's face in a particular way, she looked briefly but uncannily like *him*, despite being small for her age with delicate features and eyes as blue and soft as hydrangeas, while he had been large and his eyes cold when he…

Don't go there.

Quickly, Bella used a trick she employed when she was having trouble getting to sleep at night, something that happened too frequently lately because of the current precarious status of her job as a public relations expert and event planner at one of the biggest PR firms in Regina, Saskatchewan.

They had recently driven through the small town of Trydale, Saskatchewan, described in the ranch's brochures as being only a stone's throw away and complete with all the amenities. To calm her racing thoughts, Bella mentally listed what she had noticed driving through.

A coffee shop, a post office, a department store, a police station, a town hall...

Lily stirred and murmured something, and the shadow fell away, leaving only her daughter's face.

Bella's heart clenched with fierce protectiveness. She wanted—no she *needed*—this summer to be one that would bring Lily out of the almost reclusive shyness that had only worsened over the past school year to the point that her teachers had suggested that Bella might want to consider a specialized school.

Lily had always been an introvert, but she did have one or two close friends, and she was a great conversationalist with a sense of humor when she was comfortable.

Lately, though, her teachers complained that she wasn't participating in class and avoided talking with the other students as much as she could.

Bella wished she knew why but was also afraid that she did.

Lily had been asking more questions about her father, and Bella wondered if her refusal to provide information was somehow tied to her daughter's behavior.

Bella's phone rang into the silence of the car, startling her and causing Lily's eyes to fly open. Her expression was reproachful as it always was when she first woke up.

The ringtone told her it was her boss, and with a sigh and an apologetic look in Lily's direction, Bella eased the car to a stop at the side of the road and answered the call. It was easier to get it over with than it was to deal with persistent calls and messages.

And what Felicity Bond wanted, Bella knew, was a commitment that she was in no way ready to make and doubted she ever would be.

"Hey," Felicity said, and with that one brief word, Bella could picture her, leading the pack despite being eight years younger than Bella's own thirty-five years, her brown eyes snapping with an almost frenetic energy behind her stylish horned-rimmed glasses, her short hair gelled into spikes, her voice getting louder, her arm gestures more extravagant as she pushed them through yet another deadline and onto the next.

"Sorry, I know you're on your way to that ranch thingy," Felicity continued, with no apology in her tone. "I just wanted to remind you that you promised me you'd use this time off to do some serious thinking about your future with us."

As if I need reminding...

"If it had been anyone else who'd had a meeting with such a potentially lucrative client end so badly," Felicity continued, all pretense gone of caring about interrupting the start of Bella's summer off. "We wouldn't even be having this conversation— you'd be looking for employment elsewhere. But you've always done such great work, Bella, and I really feel that if you could just be a teeny bit flexible, you'd realize how great this could be for all of us."

"I'm not going to design a campaign that promises things that I know Jed Martin isn't capable of delivering," Bella said for what felt like the hundredth time.

They had been through this. Jed, an intimidatingly handsome entrepreneur, with more money than scruples, wanted a campaign designed around a series of books, audio books and live presentations that guaranteed that by following his steps people could become millionaires within a year.

She wouldn't be party to creating that kind of misleading campaign for anyone, let alone someone who reminded her so much of *him*.

"Bella, no one is asking you to lie," Felicity said in her impatient patient voice. "We're just asking you to consider the potential. You can do that, can't you? It would be so easy to give the campaign to someone else, but Jed has his heart set on you."

The unfortunate choice of words caused Bella to involuntarily flinch.

Lily was fully awake now and watching her mom. She pushed her light brown bangs off of her high forehead and frowned.

Bella mouthed "I'm sorry" to her and made a whirling finger gesture to indicate that she would wrap up the call as soon as she could.

"Felicity, I said I would think about it, although I don't expect to change my mind," Bella said. How could she when it went against what she believed in? "You agreed I could have until the end of August to decide what my next move was."

"I did," Felicity agreed reluctantly, "and I hope I don't end up regretting it. I know it's only the beginning of July, but time's going to go faster than you expect. I hope that while you're making the decision you realize that finding work at a new firm at the level you're at isn't going to be easy. It goes without saying that you won't be able to count on my recommendation if things don't work out here."

"I understand that," Bella said. "Thank you for giving me this time."

It took effort to stay polite and professional when she wondered how Human Resources would view her boss's borderline threatening remarks.

The pressure inherent in the call caused an accompanying pressure between Bella's eyes, but she wasn't going to raise Lily with the habit of shared prayer and family devotions before breakfast every morning and then turn around and do something she knew was wrong.

She could only hope and pray that God would reward her loyalty to principles in some way because, the truth was, she needed to stay employed one way or the other. She had a daughter who depended on her.

"Was that Felicity again?" Lily asked. Her voice was still gravelly with sleep.

"It was," Bella acknowledged. She tried to always be honest and straightforward with her daughter, except for one thing: she would never tell Lily the truth about her father.

She reached out and smoothed down Lily's bangs.

"It's going to be all right," she said, answering the question in Lily's anxious eyes.

"Are you going to lose your job, Mom?" Lily started tugging on her lower lip.

"Lily," Bella said. "I will always take care of you. You never need to worry about that."

That was the truth even if she didn't know how she was going to do it if she lost her job.

But for now, Bella was going to focus on what Lily needed and how spending the summer with these horses could help release her from whatever held her back.

Lily had always loved horses, and Bella had used that love to persuade her that summer on a ranch could be fun.

She prayed they would both find the answers they were looking for.

"There's a horse, hoof needs looking at," Cal Wayman said to Luke Duffy, and Luke wondered again if he was imagining the challenge in the ranch hand's eyes. "In stall seven in the barn."

Of course I'm imagining it. I haven't given anyone any reason to suspect the truth.

He quickly ran options through his mind. He could ask Cal to check it out—after all, he was still the boss—or he could suggest Cal delegate the task to someone else.

Or he could face the task himself.

What was the worst that could happen? The horse might kick him?

Or it might go completely ballistic like that one did when I was fourteen and leave me glad to be alive.

In his world, though, "get back up on the horse that threw you" was more than just a pithy saying, it was a way of life. So Luke never told anyone that he'd never fully recovered from the incident and remained afraid of horses to this day.

He could only imagine what his late father, Sylvester "Sly" Duffy, would have to say about that, none of it good.

Not that his father had ever flattered him or indicated he was proud of him.

"Are you gonna check it out or what?" Cal asked again. His face was hidden in the shadow of his cowboy hat, but Luke could imagine a mocking expression.

"I'm going." he said tersely.

Cal never made it a secret that he didn't have the same kind of respect for Luke as he'd had for Sly, or even for Luke's older brother, Brett, so Luke often asked himself why he didn't fire him. But Cal knew everything about the ranch and the horses, and there was no doubt that he was a valuable asset, so most of the time Luke chose to take the good and ignore the bad.

He prayed to God several times daily to give him the patience to do so.

Brett was a rising oil man in Calgary, Alberta, but still

made the occasional visit to New Hope and had strong opinions about its future.

Unfortunately, his dominant opinion was that it was time to sell, and their mother, Nora, tended to agree with him. But she hadn't been the same since the relatively recent death of her strong, take-charge husband, and Luke suspected that she was only agreeing to a sale because she couldn't envision another solution.

He was determined, though, to make them realize that the ranch was worth saving. He had never managed to make his father proud while Sly Duffy was alive, but he could do this much to honor the man's legacy.

So, right now the place was bleeding money, and he had no real idea how to make that stop. The guest cabins could use some serious sprucing, and the furnace in the large ranch house where he and his mother lived was on its last legs. Luke loved every bit of the place, the changeable sky above it and the earth below it, with a deep and lasting kind of love.

There was no way he was going to sell it, especially not to the Cooper brothers, who had a reputation for cheating at the rodeo that was held every summer and for pushing their horses beyond what was kind. Still, they kept persisting, and Brett and their mother seemed only able to see how the money could solve their immediate problems and not what they would be giving up.

Luke even loved the horses…from a distance.

But now, with Cal watching him, he strode in the direction of the barn, gritting his teeth, watching his long legs take strides like they actually believed he wanted to go where he was going.

"Luke, hey, Luke!"

"That's Uncle Luke to you," he said under his breath and

turned in the direction of the voice that came from his thir-teen-year-old niece, Alison.

Alison was Brett and his wife Gwen's daughter, left at the ranch while her parents took what Gwen insisted on referring to as a "healing holiday" for the sake of their marriage, which had recently hit rocky ground.

Maybe what their marriage needed was for both of them to be home more, focused on each other and on Alison instead of on their careers, Luke often thought.

Then again, he wasn't the biggest fan of much they did since he had dated Gwen first, and she had dumped him as soon as Brett showed signs of being a more lucrative provider.

Their mother wasn't up to dealing with a teenager, espe-cially one who wasn't happy to be spending her summer with them, so the responsibility had fallen to Luke.

If possible, he felt less up to the task than his mother did, but what was he going to do? He couldn't desert Alison. He was sure—well, almost sure—that behind the face of makeup that he was repeatedly telling her to wash off and the insolent attitude, there beat the heart of a girl who just needed to know she hadn't been totally abandoned.

Although now, with her swaggering toward him, wearing cutoff jean shorts and a T-shirt of some band he didn't know and didn't want to, Luke second-guessed his assumptions.

Still, although he didn't appreciate the way she delivered them, the next words out of her mouth were a welcome re-prieve.

"Hey, Luke, Grandma says that guests have arrived, and she needs you to go up to the house to sign them in."

"It's *Uncle* Luke," he said automatically. He turned back to Cal, who had, for his own reasons, ambled along behind. "You heard it," Luke said, trying to sound like the boss who had every right to give an order and not like someone whose knees were about to buckle with relief. "I'm heading up to the house, so you'll have to look in on the horse and report back to me."

Cal touched the brim of his hat so solemnly he couldn't be accused of disrespect—but still...

"Come with me?" Luke suggested to Alison. "See who the new arrivals are."

Alison shrugged but followed him up to the house.

Inside the lobby of the large ranch house, an attractive woman with dark blond hair waited with a girl who appeared to Luke to be a few years younger than Alison.

His eyes took in the woman and drew an immediate conclusion: one hundred percent city. He knew the type. A royal blue blouse that looked like it would need dry cleaning if the slightest spot marred it, blue jeans stiff with newness. At least her shoes didn't have heels on them.

Her hair was shoulder-length and carefully groomed, her eyes a piercing blue with a speculative expression as she took in the surroundings.

The only thing was that usually this type came with a new boyfriend they were trying to impress, playing cowboy and cowgirl all weekend, or with a group of girlfriends of a similar type.

But this one was with her daughter, who was chewing on the end of her long brown braid. At least, he assumed it was her daughter. They had similar bone structure and delicate features.

Alison snorted and then made wide, innocent eyes when the others looked at her.

"Lily," the woman said, in a tone far gentler than Luke would have expected. "Your hair."

Luke felt like he was intruding on something, also that the woman was holding herself back from getting in Alison's face.

A fierce protective instinct on behalf of his difficult niece rose up within him. No doubt the same one that caused the woman's pretty features to briefly scrunch into something feral.

Then he cleared his throat and reminded himself that these were much-needed guests.

He went behind the desk that was set up in the foyer and flipped open a large book.

"What brings you to New Hope?" he asked. There, that sounded pretty good. He hardly sounded at all like he was wondering how much time he could get away with *not* being in this woman's presence.

"Before we sign in…"

"Yes?" Luke looked up from the book, already sensing he wasn't going to like whatever she planned to say.

"Are the cabins—I don't really know how to ask this, so I'm just going to ask."

Of course you are.

"Are the cabins cleaned on a regular basis?"

"Mom!"

So the braid-chewer had a voice and was using it to express intense embarrassment with a single syllable.

Luke didn't even want to look at Alison.

"Yes, they are." He answered the question, and that was all he needed to do. But then he couldn't resist adding, "Why do you ask?"

"They just look a little…unkempt, at least from the outside. A fresh coat of paint would really spruce things up," she added helpfully.

Now, instead of saying anything, the daughter tugged frantically on her mother's hand and went up on her toes to whisper something in her mother's ear.

Whatever she said caused a kind of sad softness to spread over the woman's features. It was a look that Luke didn't understand entirely but somehow understood far too well.

"We'll sign in now," she said. "My name is Arabella Lark, and this is my daughter, Lily."

Luke hesitated briefly then picked up a pen.

These were guests, he reminded himself, and the ranch needed guests.

Even ones that had already caused his insides to do a dance filled with missteps.

Chapter Two

Despite the worn exterior of the cabin they were staying in, the interior was clean, as that Luke Duffy had promised. In fact, it was polished to a shine as if someone had taken pride in doing so. The gloss of the dark hardwood floor with the circular braided rug in multicolors on it, the flowered quilts on the bed and the starched curtains at the window, all contributed to an atmosphere of old-fashioned charm.

Bella watched Lily take it all in, and a small smile lifted the corners of her mouth. She let her breath out in a gentle gust.

Luke hadn't seemed very pleased when she questioned the cleanliness of the cabins. Well that was his problem. If anyone hoped to make a success of their business, they would soon learn to welcome the feedback of paying customers, even if most of them didn't have the expertise in marketing and public relations that she did.

But she was here for Lily's sake and to give herself some time and space to figure out what her next move was going to be. Her best friend and business associate, Emery Forsythe, had recommended this place when Bella had confided some of the struggles she was having, and Emery had never steered her wrong, so Bella was determined to make the most of their time here.

In their cabin that evening, they unpacked and then read for a while, occasionally interrupting the silence to make comments to each other about their books.

Later, Lily fell easily asleep but sleep eluded Bella.

She wanted to have as little to do with Luke Duffy as possible.

The scowl she had seen on his face was still etched behind her eyelids every time she closed her eyes to try to sleep. So she had no idea why she couldn't stop thinking that, without the scowl, he'd be a handsome man with those eyes as changeable as the prairie sky, thick dark brown hair and strong jaw.

The sun rather than her alarm clock woke Bella up the next morning, and she couldn't remember the last time that had happened. The bed was comfortable, like the warm hug of an oversized grandmother, and when she had finally fallen asleep, her sleep had been deep and solid.

She sat up and pushed her hair out of her eyes. Across the room, Lily was already dressed in blue jeans and a pink-and-blue plaid shirt, and she was coaxing her long hair into its usual braid.

"Hey, Lil." Bella glanced at her phone, trying to register the time without being bothered by all the text messages, most of them from Felicity.

Her boss gave good lip service to giving Bella time and space to figure things out, but it didn't show in her actions.

Bella reached for her purse and firmly tucked the phone inside, making sure to silence it.

"How did you sleep?" she asked Lily.

"Good."

Bella was about to start speculating on how their day would unfold when there was a knock at the door.

Bella and Lily exchanged glances, and Bella pulled her housecoat on over her pajamas and opened the door.

The young girl from the night before stood outside, and

Bella couldn't help immediately contrasting her height and maturing figure, which she dressed to enhance, with her daughter's petite frame.

She'd be prettier without the make-up, she thought.

She regretfully noticed Lily making the same comparison. She knew that her daughter was self-conscious about being smaller and looking younger than other girls her age, and Bella wished Lily knew how pretty she was.

In a familiar gesture of insecurity, Lily reached for her braid then jammed her hands in her pockets instead.

"Can we help you?" Bella asked the girl at the door.

For a second, the girl appeared taken aback by Bella's crisp tone but quickly recovered herself. "Luke says to come up to the house for breakfast, and then he'll get one of the ranch hands to give you a tour of the place."

"You call your father by his first name?" It was none of her business, but Bella couldn't help herself.

"He's my uncle," the girl replied, and Bella imagined her restraining an eye roll.

"Okay…well, thank you." Bella was *not* going to get into a battle of wills with this girl, whatever her problem was. As long as she didn't do anything to upset Lily's time here, they could all exist in the same environment.

Bella put on her own jeans and a plaid shirt, hers in shades of aqua. On impulse, she quickly braided her own hair. It wasn't a style she would ever wear to the office, which was exactly why it felt right.

Despite its somewhat intimidating size, the main house initially had the same warm and cozy feel as the cabins, with hardwood floors polished to a high gleam, scattered braided rugs everywhere Bella could see and furnishings that looked both plush and lived in. The pictures on the wall summed up both a love for nature and a family history.

In one, Bella was sure she spotted a young Luke, his blue eyes intense and his smile slightly challenging.

It was a beautiful and comfortable space, but with the home being considerably larger than the cabins, it was also easier to see more areas where things needed touching up.

"I think it must be this way," Bella murmured, following the smell of food and the murmur of low chatter. Somewhat to her surprise, she was hungry, and the smells were tantalizing.

Lily suddenly froze in the doorway leading into the kitchen.

Bella peered past her and saw a long table with bench seats surrounding it, covered by a red-and-white checked tablecloth, on which there were stacks of pancakes, plates of sausage, bacon and scrambled eggs, pitchers of orange and apple juice and carafes of coffee.

Wherever they were cutting corners, she mused, it didn't appear to be with the food they were serving the guests.

Around the table sat Luke, the girl who claimed he was her uncle and an older woman who wore a pensive expression and had a fragile beauty like a precious china ornament that hadn't been dusted in some time.

If there were other guests, there were no signs of them.

Lily cleared her throat, returning Bella's attention to her. She had been distracted by the riches of food, her rumbling stomach and the sight of that Luke person pouring coffee for that older woman—his mother, likely—wearing an expression of tenderness.

She leaned down slightly and took both of Lily's hands in hers.

"Doesn't everything look and smell delicious?" she encouraged. "I know there are a few other people there, but you and I will sit together and visit, and after breakfast we'll probably get to see the horses."

She had no idea if that was true, but she hoped it was.

"What if they ask me a bunch of questions?" Lily fretted.

Bella stole a glance at the table. "I think they've got their own things on their minds," she ventured.

She squeezed Lily's hands and prayed silently that all would be well.

It could have been Lily's own appetite or her eagerness to see the horses, but in any case, she agreed to enter the room for breakfast.

"Good morning," Luke greeted them. "Please sit wherever you like."

Bella and Lily chose to sit across from him and his niece. The older woman sat at the head of the table but, somehow, didn't quite look like she belonged there.

"Let's give thanks for the food," Luke said. He recited what sounded like a memorized grace.

"I'm Luke Duffy," he introduced himself again after the prayer.

Playing host, Bella noted, but not like it came naturally to him.

"This is my niece, Alison."

The girl glanced up from her scrambled eggs and gave them a halfhearted salute with her fork.

"And this is my mother, Nora Duffy."

"It's lovely you could be here," Nora said, her voice deeper and richer than Bella would have imagined.

Bella gestured to herself and then to Lily. "Arabella and Lily Lark, but please call me Bella," she added habitually.

"Arabella? That's a funny name," Alison noted, ignoring the "don't embarrass us" hand signals her uncle was sending her.

Bella fought an urge to burst into laughter.

"It was the name of one of my great aunts," she said, "and, no, it isn't one you hear much anymore."

"Lily is a pretty name," Luke said. No doubt he just wanted

to change the subject, but the glance he gave her shy daughter was particularly gentle.

"And what brings you here to New Hope?" Nora asked smoothly, the inherent sadness Bella thought she'd seen masked by a veneer of civility.

Bella knew the type. She had seen many a wife of a lucrative client who excelled at social graces. But there was no husband in sight now, and the woman radiated a powerful aura of loss.

"A good friend of mine recommended you," she answered. "Emery Forsythe writes an online blog on hidden gems on the Canadian prairies, and she did a feature on your ranch and also personally recommended it to me. She thought it would be good for…"

Under the table, Lily's knee firmly bumped against hers.

"Good for us city girls to learn something new," she amended.

"Your plaid shirts are adorable," Alison said, widening her hazel eyes. "Did you get those especially for coming here?"

"Alison," Luke said warningly, but Bella met the girl's gaze square on.

"We did," she said. "I appreciate you noticing them."

"A few plaid shirts in your own wardrobe might be more suitable than what you choose to wear," Nora said, and Alison's ears flamed red.

Bella was instantly regretful. She hadn't meant to start anything, and she knew she'd better steer the conversation quickly in another direction before breakfast became more than Lily could handle.

"Your hair is lovely, Alison," she said. It really was, with its rich auburn shade. "Is that natural wave?"

Alison nodded, mumbled thanks and returned her attention to her scrambled eggs.

"You must be hungry," Luke said, clearly relieved that the moment had passed. He hoisted one of the plates. "Would you like sausage or bacon, or both?"

Soon, Bella and Lily were enjoying their breakfast, and the strong, rich coffee was doing its work to prepare Bella for the day ahead.

"Alison's mother has the most stunning red hair herself," Nora said conversationally, and Bella didn't know if she saw or imagined Luke's hand tremble slightly as he served himself another pancake.

"Her parents are traveling," Nora continued, "and she's spending the summer with us and perhaps longer. Isn't that right, Alison?"

"That's right, Gran," Alison said flatly. Then she turned to Lily and, with the kind of deliberateness of someone wanting to steer attention away from herself, asked, "Where's your dad?"

Luke didn't see if it was Bella's or Lily's hand that upset the glass of orange juice, but suddenly spilled juice was spreading over the tablecloth, and they all instinctively pushed their chairs back and jumped up.

"I'm so sorry," Bella moaned. "Is there any paper towel or rags I can use to clean it up?"

"No worries," Luke said, grabbing the napkins that were in reach to stop the worst of the spill before hurrying off for other cleaning supplies.

When he returned, Bella held out her hand and told him with a look not to argue, so he handed her a cloth, and she began sopping up fluid.

Lily meanwhile slouched in her hair, tugging agitatedly at her braid, while Alison placidly gnawed a corner of toast and his mother seemed to have returned, with an expression of vague puzzlement, to a world of her own.

I can only imagine what you'd have to say about this, Dad.

Luke had no doubt that his father would want more of him than to see him leaping about cleaning up orange juice spills.

Bella went to the sink to rinse and vigorously ring out the cloth she had used.

She wasn't afraid to pitch in, Luke noted. He also couldn't help noticing that the plaid shirt and blue jeans and her braided hair gave her a softer look than the one she'd had when he met her.

But he wasn't in the least interested in her except as a paying guest, so it was time to move the day along.

He joined her at the sink to rinse out his own dishcloth.

"As soon as you and your daughter are ready," he said, "I'll get one of the ranch hands to take you to the horses and explain some of the things we do here."

He thought it was funny, yet somehow not amusing at all, the way he could still make it sound like there was a whole team of workers at the ready to choose from. That may have been the case when Sly Duffy was still in charge of things, but now Cal was the obvious and best choice.

Except Luke didn't think Cal would be too keen on doing it, and, what was more, he wasn't too keen on him taking on the task, though he wasn't sure why.

He just couldn't escape a sensation that Alison's question about Lily's father had triggered a reaction and not a positive one.

But once again he reminded himself that he was trying to run a business and not to get involved in the personal lives of guests.

Still, he found himself saying, "Actually, I'll tell you

what. I'll take you over to the horses myself." He ignored his mother's soft blink of surprise and Alison's eye roll.

Of course, he had made sure that no one in his family actually knew he was afraid of the horses. Even if they might suspect it, he would never confirm it for them, and most of the time his attention was better needed elsewhere.

"How about I meet you outside your cabin in about half an hour?" he said.

Bella glanced at Lily, who nodded, and she said, "Okay, sounds like a plan."

It will be fine.

After they departed, Luke continued to help with kitchen cleanup, urging Alison to pitch in. She did so but with the body language and facial expression of someone making an enormous personal sacrifice.

Meanwhile, his mother had poured herself another cup of coffee and said, "I'll be reading in my room if anyone needs me."

She carried a book under her arm, but it was the same book she'd had tucked under her arm for months, and Luke knew that her "reading" time would more than likely consist of her staring at the portrait of Sly that graced their bedroom wall or flipping through the many photo albums of pictures that captured their lives together.

Luke suppressed a sigh. It wouldn't do his mother any good to know how sad he was for her, or how discouraged about the future of their ranch.

He would figure something out.

I have to.

As arranged, Luke waited outside the Larks' cabin half an hour later. He was happy he had used the extra elbow grease needed to clean it to a shine, particularly after Bella had questioned the cleanliness of the place.

While he waited, he did his best to convince himself that he'd do just fine with the horses. The therapy horses were the gentlest of all the horses on the ranch. They were specially trained to interact well with people who struggled with phobias or who were recovering from physical or emotional trauma. At least, that was what he remembered from when they purchased the horses from a couple in Alberta who were retiring.

Maybe he should have paid a little more attention, especially since it had been his idea to spend money that wasn't easy to come by to inject some additional income into New Hope, but he had never envisioned being in charge of them once the purchase was complete.

This made it even more puzzling that he had volunteered to take the reins, as it were, when it came to their guests.

Of course, he would do what he could to ensure any paying guests had a memorable time here. He would do whatever he could to make sure they carried away a positive experience that they were willing to share with others.

He had to admit that he was curious about this attractive woman and her shy daughter. He wondered what their expectations of the ranch were and hoped he'd be able to meet them.

Was there a husband and father in the picture?

As they walked to the stable where the therapy horses were kept, Luke watched Bella taking in her surroundings in a way that made him visualize her taking notes.

He thought he heard her murmur something about the place having a lot of potential.

"I'm sorry, what?" he asked.

She looked a bit startled that she'd voiced her thought. "Oh, I was just thinking that a few improvements and some good promotion could really get this place off the ground."

Off the ground?

Bella hadn't known the ranch in its glory days, under the

sure hands of the incomparable Sly Duffy, but still the words stung.

"I don't believe in advertising," Luke retorted. "Word of mouth does the trick just as well. You're here, aren't you?"

Bella turned a steady gaze in his direction.

"Yes, that's because I trusted the word of someone who's been my best friend for years, someone whose judgment I know I can trust. I don't see other guests around."

There was no malice in her words. She was a straight shooter, and Luke had the thought that his father would have appreciated that.

He wasn't sure, though, how he felt about it.

But they arrived at the stables, and he was saved from having to think of an appropriate answer.

Lily gave a small skip of happiness then stumbled a little as if embarrassed by the action.

She did seem so much younger than Alison, and yet Luke didn't really believe that Alison was happy with the grown-up role she was playing.

"Now take things slowly," he heard Bella reminding Lily. "Let Mr. Duffy take the lead."

Well, that's a good one.

"Yes," Luke said as he entered the stables, trying to make it look like his slow amble was emulating a famous movie cowboy and not a show of reluctance. "The important thing is," he continued, quoting from the pamphlets he'd inexpertly made, "that you give it time. You might not know right away which horse you'll work best with, and that's okay."

Bella slid him a look that told him that she recognized exactly where he was getting his spiel from.

"Anyway," he ad-libbed, "ready to meet the horses?"

Lily nodded. The smile that lit her face brought a true beauty to it.

As Luke approached the first stall, he could feel them following closely behind him. He didn't know if the summer meadow scent that emanated from Bella was her perfume or some kind of soap. He just knew that he found it a not unpleasant distraction.

But it was still a distraction he didn't need.

He paused at the first stall. The horse had its nose in a bucket of oats but lifted it up when he heard their approach. He was a fine-looking horse, a deep chestnut color with a blaze of autumn gold running across his face.

He made himself breathe slowly in and out. *He'll know I'm afraid.*

Horses were extraordinarily sensitive to moods, which was only one of the things that made them perfect therapy animals.

But the horse swept his gaze past all of them, snorted a little and returned to his feast.

"Okay, this one is Hooligan," Luke said, as Lily stepped closer to get a better look.

"Careful, Lily," Bella said. "That's quite the name." She attempted a casual laugh, but Luke could tell that her own nerves had come into play.

His need to reassure her was suddenly stronger than his own apprehension. Maybe it was her city-girl attempt to look country in her plaid shirt, or maybe it was the way soft tendrils of hair were already escaping her braid.

"I think whoever named this one had a sense of irony," he said. "The truth is that if there was such a thing as a good cup of horse coffee, this guy could use some to really get going."

Bella burst out laughing, and Luke experienced a surge of pleasure.

"Joking aside," he said, returning to all business because there was no way he needed to be thinking of her as anything other than a guest. "All of these horses are specially chosen and trained to be good with people, so I'm sure you have nothing to worry about, despite the name."

If he kept this up, he might even be able to convince himself.

"We should have brought a carrot or an apple," he said. He would remember next time and maybe a few lumps of sugar.

Why am I planning for next time? This isn't what I do.

"Your daughter's very shy," Luke ventured quietly when Lily was fully immersed in trying to coax Hooligan over to see her.

"She's fine," Bella said shortly in a way that told Luke that she'd answered to this more times than she cared to.

"There's nothing wrong with that," he hurried to say. "She seems like a great kid. Honestly, I don't know what's up with Alison and I wish I understood her better and knew how to help."

Now he had definitely said too much. Alison staying with them was his family's business. He didn't need to confess his feelings of incompetency to someone he barely knew.

But Bella's face had softened.

"It's a tough age, for sure," she said. "She's about thirteen, fourteen?"

He nodded. "She's thirteen."

"Lily is twelve, so my turn soon."

Luke refrained from saying that he would have guessed Lily to be younger than that and also from saying that he doubted teenage Lily would be anything like teenage Alison.

He couldn't help thinking that Bella had the aura of secrecy around her, like she was never going to let anyone get too close. He wondered why that was.

Well, whatever it was, he didn't have the time or the inclination to get too deeply involved. They were here as guests and his job was to make sure their experience here met their expectations.

He clapped his hands together in a gesture much more decisive than he felt, like he knew what was supposed to come next.

Startled by the noise, Hooligan reared up his head and rushed toward where Lily stood.

Chapter Three

Bella shrieked and a primal mother's instinct propelled her toward her daughter. She put her hands firmly on Lily's shoulders and yanked backward, setting them both off balance. They teetered together for a few seconds like dizzily spinning tops but managed to right themselves.

"Are you okay?" she gasped. Maybe that name Hooligan wasn't such a joke after all

Lily nodded. "Luke scared him," she said rather accusingly. "It's okay, Hoolie," she called over to the horse, whose sides heaved while he gave Luke the side-eye. "You're a good boy," she added.

Despite the scare, Bella shook her head and laughed. This was the side of her daughter that others rarely got to see. Yes, she was shy, but when something mattered to her, she would take a stand.

She guessed that Lily wouldn't want to meet the other horses and had already decided that Hooligan—or "Hoolie" as she had nicknamed him—would be the horse she claimed as hers while they were there. He would be the one she learned to groom, to interact with, to ride if she chose. By doing so, she would learn to know her own mind, learn to trust herself and become more confident.

Or so New Hope Ranch promised.

Luke.

Bella suddenly remembered the rancher and wondered why he hadn't stepped in. She turned to him and saw him gripping his phone, a grim expression on his face.

In all of the commotion, she hadn't heard it ring. She was torn between anger that he wasn't paying more attention to what had just happened and concern because the look in his stormy blue eyes clearly signaled that he wasn't happy with whatever he was hearing.

He caught Bella's eyes on him and ended the call.

"Is she okay?" He tilted his head in Lily's direction. "Sorry about that," he added. "I had to take that call."

"You scared the horse with your clapping," Lily said.

"I did," he acknowledged. "That was a bad move on my part, and I hope it won't discourage you from giving us both another chance."

Okay, point for the rancher, Bella thought, respecting his no-excuses directness.

"It won't," Lily said. Then, as Bella had already guessed she would, she said, "I think I'd like to work with Hooligan while I'm here."

"Are you sure?" Luke glanced again at his phone but then put it back into the pocket of his blue jeans.

"That looked important," Bella said, pointing at the pocket. "Is there something you need to get to?"

"A few more minutes isn't going to make a difference at this point," Luke said. "To tell you the truth, it's not something I want to deal with at all."

He clamped his mouth shut like he knew he'd said too much and turned his attention back to Lily.

"You haven't even met the other horses," he reminded her.

"Your pamphlet says when you know, you know," she reminded him. "Hoolie and I just know."

"Hoolie?" He leveled a look at Bella.

"What are you looking at me for?" She laughed.

"Okay, Hoolie," Luke said. "Your new friend will be back to learn about you soon. In the meantime, I do have to get a meeting over with. You're welcome up at the house, I'm sure. There's always coffee on in the kitchen, and we have a decent library. It was actually…" Something hitched in his voice that caused Bella's heart to twinge in return. Luke swallowed, and when he spoke again his voice was stronger. "Collecting books was a bit of a passion for my father," he said. "Though, he would have told you himself that he was usually too busy to actually read them."

"The best books are like friends," Bella observed.

Luke looked for a moment like he was going to say more, but then an invisible curtain fell over his face, and he said, "I'd better take you back up."

As they walked from the barn back up toward the house, Bella watched Lily walking beside Luke and heard her asking a few questions about Hooligan. She knew it wasn't all that unusual for Lily to forget her shyness if a strong interest in something trumped it, and she also knew she should be pleased to see that her daughter wasn't having any trouble talking to Mr. Duffy. Helping Lily overcome whatever inner barriers she had set up was why they were here, after all.

But the truth was she didn't know how she felt.

In theory, Bella would have said that, of course, she wanted Lily to believe and trust that there were good men in the world. But the reality was that, since she wasn't sure she would ever truly believe that herself, it was difficult to convey that wish to her daughter.

She knew all too well that people could appear to be something they weren't.

He was charming and popular, fun to be with, a gentleman in every way…

Until he wasn't.

She marveled now that she had been naïve enough to think that if you knew someone in common, it must mean your date was a good and trustworthy guy.

She'd been set up with *him* by an acquaintance from work when she'd expressed a desire to date again, after breaking up with her high school sweetheart.

Later, she'd found out that this work acquaintance really only knew him through the friend of a friend. But, by that time, Bella wasn't saying anything to anyone about what had happened.

She'd been so eager to go on a date that she hadn't asked many questions, and there was no one to blame for that but her.

Sometimes she even considered creating some kind of mythical father figure for Lily, someone who died a heroic death before their daughter's birth, but she couldn't bring herself to do it. Not only did she never want to lie about anything—she reasoned with herself that not talking at all about Lily's father wasn't a lie—she couldn't create a fairy tale out of what had happened to her.

An only child, Bella didn't have a sister to confide in or a brother to protect her. Her parents were loving but simply not the kind of people she could take this kind of thing to, and even if she could have talked about it to them or to any of her friends, all she strove to do was to block it out of her life like it had never happened.

She was doing the best she could with Lily and making choices that she believed were in her daughter's best interests. It would have been nice, though, if sometimes there was someone to reassure her that she was doing the right thing.

When they arrived back at the house, Luke offered to show them the library.

"Or do you want to get something to drink first?" he asked.

"We can find our way around the kitchen," Bella told him.

She wished he would just leave and go do whatever it was he had to do. Lily's comfort level with him, uncanny in such a short time, and the sense that he had problems deeper than he wanted to talk about—just as she did—wasn't settling well with her.

She had no idea what was going on with him, she told herself. Still, her ability to get a sense of people, and to be right more often than not, was one of the reasons she was so good at her job.

Nora hurried out from whatever she'd been doing.

"They're in Sly's office," she said by way of greeting. "They're waiting for you."

Luke's mouth twisted like he tasted sour milk.

"This won't take long," he said firmly.

"Luke." Nora wrung her hands. "If you would just…"

"Mom." Luke didn't allow her to continue. "If you would be so good as to see if our guests want something to drink and point them to the library, this won't take long."

Bella was sure that it was years of practice that helped Nora regain her hosting manners and turn to them with a smile.

"Of course," she said. "It would be my pleasure."

Soon, Bella and Lily had glasses of lemonade and were following Nora down a hallway.

They passed a closed door, and Bella heard the rumble of male voices. She couldn't make out any words, but the timbre wasn't friendly.

What's going on here?

As Luke had promised, the library was a book lover's haven, and soon Lily was engrossed in a well-worn copy of *My Friend Flicka*. Her lemonade was in reach but neglected as she turned pages.

Bella tried to interest herself in a vintage women's magazine, but she couldn't concentrate. She kept speculating on what the tension between Luke Duffy and his mother was about because clearly there was something going on.

She stole a glance at Lily, who was absent-mindedly giving her braid gentle little tugs while she read.

If they had landed in the middle of some kind of family crisis, should they stay out the summer here? And if they didn't, what were their other options?

Whatever was going on, Lily seemed unbothered by it, and she was the main reason they were here in the first place. She had already taken a shine to one of the horses, and she was comfortable with Luke.

So should they just wait it out and see what happened over the next few days?

Please, Lord, help me make the best decision.

Prayer was good, and Bella certainly believed in it, but once again she thought that sometimes it would be nice to have a partner—a father figure for Lily—to talk things over with.

But she still doubted she would ever trust a man that much.

Sooner than she expected, there was a tap on the outside frame of the door, and Luke poked his head in.

He smiled but looked weary, Bella thought.

"How's it going here, ladies?" he asked. "Content where you are, or would you like to start learning more about the horses?"

"Horses." Lily cast the book aside without hesitation.

Nora came up behind Luke.

"Luke, you're not done with your meeting already, are you?" Her attempt to speak in a hushed tone didn't mask the agitation in her voice.

"Let's just say they made me an offer I found easy to refuse," Luke said flatly.

"Of all the stubborn…" Nora sputtered, unmindful of their guests' presence again.

Bella cast an anxious look in Lily's direction, but her daughter looked curious and showed no signs of crawling back into her protective shell.

"Mom, please." Luke's voice remained calm but held a strong warning note.

"If your father was here…" Nora's tirade continued, but the details of it faded as Luke propelled her down the hallway.

"I'll be right back," he said over his shoulder. "Don't worry, everything is fine."

But Bella couldn't help wondering if those were famous last words.

Back in the kitchen, Luke dropped all pretense of a jovial exterior.

"Mom, what is the matter with you? We have guests in the house, *paying* guests, and they don't need to hear our family issues."

"There wouldn't be any issues, Lucas, if you would do the reasonable thing and agree to sell this place." Nora gripped his forearms with maternal strength, and her eyes pleaded with him. "I know it's what your father would have wanted."

"Do you really think that?" Luke said, raw pain cutting through him. "Mom, if you remember Dad and love him the way I know you did, I don't think you can honestly believe that."

He paused and took a breath that was a brief prayer for the right words.

"This ranch meant everything to him," he said. "Next to family, I don't think there was anything that was more important to Dad. I can't—I won't—accept that he would want us selling the ranch, let alone to people like the Coopers."

"Well, we'll see what your brother has to say about it when he gets home." His mother turned her back to him and made a pretense of plugging the kettle in for tea, but her shoulders were tense up around her ears.

"Mom," Luke said, not wanting to plead. "I know you're worried about money, and I know that Brett has convinced you that selling as quickly as you can is the fastest and best way out of the predicament. But Brett has his own things on his mind."

He paused. Despite their differences, Brett was his brother, and it wasn't in Luke's nature to throw someone under the bus when that person wasn't there to defend himself.

His mother forgot about the tea and turned back to him, her shoulders slumped in defeat.

"I just don't understand why your father would have chosen to make such a bad investment," she fretted for the umpteenth time. "It wasn't like him at all. Maybe his illness impacted his ability to make decisions. But why he would pour all that money into a town growth project that he didn't even discuss with me is something I will never understand. I can't even find record of what the project was supposed to be."

There was nothing Luke felt he could say or do except listen to his mother, once again, travel the paths of speculation.

"What's everybody doing?" Alison wandered into the kitchen, and Luke had the same pang of guilt and surprise he got whenever she resurfaced from whatever she'd been doing. He wasn't yet fully used to her being around.

He remembered that she'd been a cute, rather precocious child, but he'd always had other things on his mind during their sporadic visits and hadn't exactly been a doting uncle; though, given that her parents had basically abandoned her, he was really trying to do better.

"Our guests are in the library," he said, "if you want to find them. Maybe you and Lily can hang out or something."

"Oh, please, Luke." Alison's expression was maybe just

a degree less derisive than the one of the surly singer that graced her T-shirt. "Does that kid *look* like someone I'd hang out with?"

"Okay, then," he said in a tone he recognized as belonging to a displeased Sly Duffy. "Instead of that, how about you help me set up an Uncle Luke jar, and every time you call me Luke instead of Uncle Luke, you can donate some of your spending money. How does that sound?"

Alison's face faltered, and she was suddenly a young teenager who had been forced into a summer visit she wasn't happy about.

Luke was instantly ashamed at his lack of patience.

"Well, hopefully we can find something that you will enjoy doing this summer." he said quietly. "Now I promised our guests I'd take them back to the horses. You're welcome to join us, but no pressure."

Alison looked like she was considering the best of two bad choices.

"I guess I'll come with you." Alison shrugged.

"Lu—Uncle Luke," she asked as they walked together. "I heard you and Gran—uh—arguing before I came into the kitchen. I didn't mean to. Are you really going to sell the ranch?"

"You're selling this place?" Bella asked.

Maybe Bella and Lily had grown restless in the library because suddenly they were all face-to-face in the hallway, and Bella was studying him, waiting for an answer.

Her expression was curious, not accusatory, but still, the last thing Luke wanted was for a guest to realize they were essentially spending their hard-earned money on a vacation that could self-implode at any given moment.

There was no point being frustrated with Alison either. Her timing wasn't the best, but she had every right to be curious herself. Maybe she had memories that made her more attached to the ranch than he'd thought.

But meanwhile, there were three people staring at him now, all waiting for an answer. He decided that all he could do was speak his own truth on the matter.

"I have no intention of selling the ranch."

No matter what others might want me to do.

Not wanting to dwell on the subject, Luke led the small group to the stables.

When he found himself back with Hooligan and the other horses, he felt even more self-conscious with Alison present.

There must be someone better for this job than him, even aside from how many other tough decisions he was dealing with.

But the sun hit Bella's hair as she watched Lily chattering softly to Hooligan, motherly pride, love and protectiveness all mingled together on her face, and he simply couldn't leave them.

"Better watch it." Alison's voice intruded on his thoughts. "Hooligan bites."

"He does not bite," Luke responded immediately, hoping he was right. Hooligan's bio said he was good with all ages, and surely a biter wouldn't warrant such praise or be recommended as a therapy horse, for that matter.

Lily didn't respond but her body language showed that the words troubled her.

"I'm guessing you don't have a lot of experience with horses," Alison continued, sliding a critical look toward Lily. Bella's eyes met Luke's, but he couldn't tell if she was asking or telling him something.

Maybe a little of both.

Then he noticed Lily backing slowly away from Hooligan

into a corner of the stable. Somehow, he knew that it wasn't the horse she was shying away from but Alison.

She folded her arms across her middle, and Luke could sense her drawing into herself.

He knew he should say something to Alison, but Alison was his niece, and despite her facade and off-putting behavior, he was sure she needed him. He couldn't stand up for his guests if it meant making Alison feel unwanted.

Please, God, what am I supposed to do here?

"Give it a minute." The words coming from Bella's mouth so quickly after his prayer startled Luke. Then he looked at her and saw that she was speaking more to herself than anyone. He sensed that she was almost physically restraining herself from stepping in.

Hooligan whinnied into the tension of the silence, and another horse echoed the sound.

"He's wondering what you're doing here," Alison said. "He doesn't really like strangers around him."

"He likes me." After a few more beats of silence, the words, breathless and almost inaudible, came from Lily.

Bella nodded encouragement, and Luke wondered if she even knew she was doing it.

"That's right, Lily," she murmured. "You've got this."

"He does like you," Luke addressed Lily. "I'm sure he likes you, too," he added to Alison.

I am so bad at this.

"Hey, this time I remembered the apples." He tried to gloss over the awkwardness. He had to move things along here in a positive way before the ranch's only clients decided to turn tail and leave this place far behind.

"I practically grew up at this place," Alison mumbled. "I think I know who the horses like and don't like."

She was exaggerating, Luke knew. Visiting New Hope had

never been her mother's favorite pastime, but whether that was because of him and their past relationship or something else, he didn't want to guess.

Still, he knew exactly what Alison was doing. She was staking a claim. She was a young girl who was probably missing her parents more than she was willing to admit.

It made Luke want to protect her.

"Then maybe you could show Lily around," Luke suggested. "I'm sure you would have a lot to teach her."

He pulled out the bag he had threaded through one of his belt loops, reached into it and handed each girl an apple.

They each accepted one but didn't move.

"So, what do you say?" he urged.

Alison shrugged. "I guess." Her response had all the enthusiasm of someone scheduled for a root canal.

"How does that sound, Lil?" Bella said, sounding like she was at least trying to do her part.

Her shrug was even less enthusiastic than Alison's, and she didn't say anything.

Luke wondered how it would all work out.

But one thing was for sure; he would endure this and try a thousand more things before he would *ever* sell New Hope Ranch to the unscrupulous Coopers.

Chapter Four

Bella and Lily had arrived at the ranch on a Saturday, and at dinner on Sunday, all had agreed that Monday morning was the perfect time for Lily to officially start her sessions with Hooligan, or Hoolie, as Lily insisted on calling him.

Soon her daughter, who was determined in her quiet way, would have them all calling him that, Bella mused.

"How are you doing?" she asked Lily. Now that the actual day to start the therapy was upon them, she hoped that Lily's eagerness wouldn't give way to shyness.

Bella had never specifically told Lily that these sessions were intended to help her with what others labeled as her "issues." She had spun it as a chance for Lily to grow close to and learn about an animal that had always fascinated her, and so far that approach was working.

"I'm good," Lily said. She bounced on her heels a little as she pulled her hair up into a high, swinging ponytail, a change from the braids, and then stopped bouncing to tuck her light green T-shirt into her blue jeans.

Bella wondered if Alison's sarcastic comment about their plaid shirts had caused Lily to choose the T-shirt, but she opted not to say anything. It wasn't like Lily would admit it anyway.

What she did ask was, "Did Alison show you some interesting things yesterday? You weren't gone for very long."

After Luke had appointed his niece as a reluctant tour

guide, Bella had tamped down her intense urge to tag along to protect Lily from any potential barbs. She wanted to show Luke Duffy that she was capable of being a team player.

Her own reaction to the man was troubling to her, a distraction from the real reason they were here—for Lily—and something that impeded her decision not to get too involved with any man.

Yet, she knew there was trouble in his life, as surely as she knew there was in her own. His mother and, by the sounds of it, his brother wanted to sell the ranch, and Luke didn't want to.

Bella had grown used to reading clients during her years as a public relations expert. She knew when people had true passion for their causes and when they just saw dollar signs. She saw passion in Luke's wish to save the ranch.

It made her want to help.

"Mom," Lily said, "you asked me a question, and now you're not even listening to me."

"Sorry," Bella said automatically. Her daughter's puzzled eyes upon her reminded her that the only real reason to get involved with fixing this place was to ensure that Lily had a successful summer here.

It was definitely not to turn a certain rancher's face from stormy to sunny.

Still, she mused, maybe if she could help Nora and whoever see the potential in keeping the ranch running instead of selling it, everyone would be happier.

"Well, you didn't miss much anyway," Lily said with a rather exasperated sigh. "She showed me this tree that she said she used to climb to the top of, which, by the way, I don't believe, and she talked about how many guys at her school are in love with her."

"Which, by the way, you don't believe either?" Bella prodded gently.

Lily gave an awkward shrug. "I just don't *care*."

Bella wondered if that was true. Lily was at the age when attention from boys became way more important than it should be. She saw her daughter's delicate beauty and knew that others who cared about Lily would see it too.

But she also knew that boys that age did gravitate toward Alison's type. Still, she had modeled a life where a man's attention and approval were unnecessary, so it was quite possible that Lily really didn't care.

"I'm ready to go," Lily said.

Bella did a quick scan of the cabin to ensure they'd left it tidy for the day and then gave herself an appraising once-over. She too had given up on the plaid shirt, choosing a blouse with a pattern of wildflowers instead, and also wore jeans.

As soon as they stepped outside, a male voice greeted them. "Howdy, ma'am."

It wasn't Luke; it was that ranch hand that she had seen lingering with a not quite friendly curiosity over Luke's encounters with them and the horses yesterday.

"Cal Wayman." The man swept off his large cowboy hat in a gesture, which along with his greeting, made Bella wonder if he was trying to act like he thought visitors to the ranch would expect.

From the corner of her eye, she saw Lily back up slightly, groping behind her to find the door of the cabin, clearly with the intention of disappearing back into it.

Bella reached out and gave her daughter's other hand a reassuring squeeze.

Lily had been looking so forward to her first official session. Bella wasn't going to let Cal ruin it for her.

"Arabella Lark," she said, not offering the option to shorten her name and using the tone she engaged when she needed to remind someone that she was all about business.

Cal's grin soured slightly, but he held on to it.

"Just came by to introduce myself," he said, "and to let you know that if there's anything you need, I'm the one to come to. I pretty much run this place."

"Oh? I was under the impression that this was Luke Duffy's ranch." Bella was not sure why, but she couldn't resist needling this man. In her opinion, at best, he erroneously figured himself to be a charmer; at worst, he was out to cause problems for Luke.

She barely knew the rancher, but already she believed that he didn't deserve or need any extra pressure in his life.

"Actually, it was his late father's ranch," Cal said, his voice a degree colder but a smile still on his face. "Luke's doing his best, no doubt about that."

The implication was clear: his best wasn't good enough.

But who was he to make that judgment? Bella wondered with a sudden flare of anger. In her career, she met all kinds of people, including some who had true heart for what they were doing but were kept in the shadows by the outward bluster of others.

She liked to help those ones whenever she had the opportunity. Though it wasn't likely that Luke wanted, or even knew he needed, her help.

Bella could feel Lily clutching her hand. Her fingers ached, but she didn't pull her hand away. Holding on was probably the only thing that kept Lily from fleeing.

It wasn't hard for her to imagine that she felt anger in the grip too. Lily already liked Luke and wouldn't appreciate Cal's attitude.

For her own reasons, as well as always wanting to demonstrate for Lily how to stand up for herself and others, Bella said, "You're entitled to your opinion, Mr.—Wayman, is it?

But my daughter and I think Luke is doing a fine job. We couldn't be happier with his work so far."

"Did I hear my name?"

Luke stepped out from a path that ran between the cabins. The studied casualness of his question made Bella wonder how long he'd been there and how much he had heard.

He looked in Cal's direction, and a thick layer of tension permeated the air.

"I was just telling Mr. Wayman—" she refused to call him by his first name "—that we think you're doing a wonderful job here."

Luke hesitated then nodded acknowledgment. "Thank you."

It was clear from his tightened jaw that, even if he hadn't heard much, he was already aware of why Bella might need to speak up for him.

He wasn't wearing a cowboy hat, although he carried one. In fact, dressed in a T-shirt himself, one that was navy blue and looked comfortably worn with washings, and blue jeans, he didn't at all resemble what someone would picture when they heard the terms *cowboy* or *rancher*.

Yet, Bella realized, he radiated a solid grounding in his surroundings, a pure love for the land that someone like Cal Wayman couldn't even touch.

"Cal, I'm sure you have better things to do than hang around the guests," Luke said. His tone substituted the word *bother* for *hang around*.

Their eyes held for a moment, and the rope of tension threatened to snap.

But then Cal lifted his hat again and said, "Have yourselves a good day."

He walked away, and Bella heard Lily woosh out a sigh.

Luke studied Bella's face like he wanted to ask more questions but just said, "Hi, Lily, ready to go?"

Lily said, "Yes." She let go of her mother's hand and stepped out from behind her.

The three of them began to walk toward the barn.

"You're coming too?" Luke asked Bella. "I mean that's fine, I just didn't know what your plans were."

"Maybe just long enough to see that she's getting along okay," Bella replied in a lowered voice.

"I understand," Luke said, and she got the impression that he really did.

Beside her, Lily strode with eagerness, and her swinging ponytail seemed to match her enthusiasm. Thankfully, their uncomfortable encounter with Cal hadn't ruined things.

"We'll start out slow," Luke said as they approached the barn. "Each day, we only do as much as you and the horse are comfortable with. Horses are extremely sensitive to our moods and will react accordingly."

Bella had the impression that, besides teaching Lily, he was reminding himself of something.

"Hoolie likes me," Lily said with a confidence that warmed Bella's heart.

"He does," Luke agreed. "But we have to keep in mind that he's an animal who is large enough to hurt us if things ever got out of hand. I'm not saying that you and he won't become the best of friends, but we always have to be aware that he's a large animal who will react with animal instinct. We always have to respect him."

They approached Hoolie, who whinnied in greeting, his ears pricked forward.

"Let's start with something we know he likes," Luke said.

He produced a carrot and handed it to Lily.

As Hoolie crunched the carrot down in his big teeth, Lily stroked him, murmuring that he was a good boy.

"She's a natural," Luke remarked to Bella. "She's already doing what I would have told her to do."

"That's great," Bella said. She assured herself of Lily's preoccupation then asked in hushed voice, "But can you explain to me how all of this will help with her shyness and anxiety?"

Luke furrowed his brow and rubbed the back of his neck.

"I think it has something to do with the confidence that comes with bonding and becoming more aware of how you're handling a situation by how the horse is reacting to you."

"You *think*?" Bella squeaked. Had she spent money when she wasn't sure she would remain employed and planned her and Lily's summer around someone who didn't know what he was doing?

Luke's face reddened slightly.

"Therapy horses are relatively new to us here," he said. "But I have every confidence in what we are doing."

Once again, he sounded like he was trying to convince himself.

Bella took a deep breath in, trying to give herself time to figure out what the right thing to do was.

But with Lily patting and chatting softly to Hoolie, she couldn't bring herself to stop to this first lesson, not when her daughter had been so looking forward to it.

Aside from that, she didn't want to believe that Luke had deliberately deceived them about his expertise.

Unfortunately, life had taught her that she could *not* always trust what she wanted to believe about others.

The last time Luke recalled inwardly squirming with such an acute sense of inadequacy was when he was pinned under his father's gaze, trying to explain—again—why he hadn't entered any of the town rodeo events.

"This family has a reputation to uphold," Sly had boomed. "Good thing your brother is bound to win most of the ribbons."

But the memory of that booming voice now faded in the light of Bella's blue eyes.

"I would never put your daughter at risk," he was compelled to add. "Or risk the reputation of this ranch."

Bella gently squeezed her bottom lip between her thumb and forefinger, brow creased in thought.

"Lily has been looking forward to this."

Lily paused her attention to the horse and spun to face them.

"Mom, you are *not* changing your mind."

It wasn't a question, and Luke cleared his throat to subdue the chuckle that wanted to bubble out.

"We'll have the session this morning," Bella said. "We'll see how it goes."

"Okay," he said. "Lily, we'll start with you putting Hoolie's bridle on him and leading him to the training area."

"Then what?" Lily asked, her eyes lit with eagerness.

"That might be all we do this morning," Luke said.

Lily's face collapsed. "Why?"

"Because," Luke said, knowing full well that he spoke the words as much or more for Bella's benefit, "we're not going to rush things. The only goal here is that both you and the horse feel safe and comfortable. Also, things that sometimes sound like they'll be easy and won't take any time will surprise you by how challenging they can be."

He could give about a hundred examples of that from his own life.

"Do you understand, Lily?" he asked.

"I guess so."

"Do you understand?" he couldn't resist asking Bella. "I'm not going to put Lily in a position where anything could hurt her."

He thought he only meant with the horse, but something

flashed across Bella's face as he said the words that made him want to protect them both from anything—or anyone—that was out there to hurt them.

He took a bridle off a hook near Hooligan's stall and handed it to Lily.

"What you want to do," he instructed, "is lift the bridle up with your right hand so the bit moves into the corner of his mouth. Then you're going to push his left ear forward under the head piece so it sits comfortably behind both of the ears. Then you'll thread the nose band through the check pieces. Make sure it lies flat against his head and then do up the buckle under his chin. Ready to give it a try?"

Lily nodded.

She approached Hoolie, chewing her lower lip in concentration. She lifted the bridle in her right hand, as she'd been instructed…and Hooligan flung his head back, shuffling slightly backward from her.

Luke found that he was holding his own breath, then reminded himself that the horse would pick up on his apprehension and made himself ease out his breath.

In many ways, the therapy horses had been good for him. Knowing that they'd been specially chosen and trained to interact with people helped curb some of the fear he experienced around horses. Still, as he'd told Lily, they were large animals and could demonstrate unpredictable behavior.

He sensed Bella's eyes on him, aware of the tension that also threaded its way through her.

What was it about her that made him want to impress her? There were so many more important reasons why he couldn't let this venture be a failure, but right now all he could think about was not failing in her eyes.

"Hoolie senses that you're not used to this," Luke said, disciplining his voice into something calm and authoritative.

"You can take a moment, if you want. In fact, take as long as you need to trust yourself that you can do this. He will sense your confidence."

Bella folded her arms across her chest, and he found himself making a concerted effort not to let his eyes linger on her. She was an attractive woman, no doubt about that, but she wasn't his type at all, even if he was looking for a type.

Which he wasn't.

"I'm ready to try again," Lily said with a note in her voice that made Luke wonder if the preteen suspected that his thoughts had strayed for a moment.

Once again, she lifted the bridle, and once again, Hooligan reared back his head.

Luke took slow breaths, sensing that beside him Bella was doing the same thing and restraining herself from saying anything.

He'd bridled a few difficult horses in his time, knowing full well that his nervousness around them wasn't helping matters, but often there just wasn't anyone around to do it.

On occasion, he'd had the oddest sensation that the horses knew he didn't want to feel that way around them and would allow him success.

"Try to maintain some gentle pressure on the head next time he withdraws," Luke urged, speaking softly. "But drop the pressure as soon as he yields. The last thing we want is to make him feel forced."

"We're fine," Lily said, not taking her eyes off the horse. "Aren't we, Hoolie?"

Hooligan whinnied softly.

"Are you ready to try this again?" she asked him.

On the third try, the bridle went on successfully.

Luke huffed out a sigh of relief then squared his shoulders as Bella's eyes darted in his direction.

"Your daughter's a horse whisperer," he told her.

He hadn't realized how much he wanted to make her smile until she did.

The smile brought a softness to her determined face that he wouldn't have expected and a beauty that he couldn't afford to linger on.

"That's a real accomplishment, Lily," Luke said. "You should be proud of yourself."

"I'm proud of Hoolie," she said. "It's not easy being around new people. Can we take him out to the training field now?"

Now that he was bridled, Hooligan let Lily lead him as if they'd been doing it together for years.

Of course, he knew that the horse had been trained and, more importantly, had a nature conducive to working well with others, but he did also believe in special connections between some animals and humans.

He wondered to whom—or what—Lily's attractive mother had a connection to.

"Your niece, Alison, wasn't at breakfast this morning" Bella said, surprising Luke as he'd assumed they wouldn't be making conversation aside from what pertained to the horse training. "I hope everything is okay."

"I think it is," Luke said, thinking that it had barely registered with him that his niece hadn't been there. If it had, he was sure that his primary emotion would have been relief. He already had so much on his mind, and her attitude challenged him when he was in no frame of mind to be challenged.

What kind of uncle did that make him? One who needed to try harder, he answered himself.

"I mean, I'm sure everything is fine," he amended, trying to sound like he knew what he was talking about. "Sometimes she just isn't hungry for breakfast. You know how teenage girls can be?"

Like he had a clue himself, but he couldn't stand the thought of Bella Lark doubting his expertise on something else.

"Hmm, I don't know about that," Bella said, her mouth upturned in amusement. "Lily is always hungry."

"Lily?" Luke couldn't help questioning. "*That* Lily?" He pointed.

Bella laughed and the sound reminded him of water dancing over the pebbles in the brook behind the house.

I must show her that sometime.

No, he had to stop thinking those kinds of thoughts. The brook, one of his favorite places for reflection, had nothing to do with why the guests were there.

"Yes, that Lily," Bella answered, imitating his tone. "Don't let her small frame fool you. That girl can pack it in."

"Huh, who would have thought?" Luke shook his head and smiled, enjoying the light conversation between them. It gave him some assurance that he had passed the first hurdle and Bella wasn't going to be in such a rush to pack up and leave.

For a moment Bella looked like she too was enjoying the unexpected bond of communication between them. Then she lifted her chin, with a determined look, and said in a businesslike voice, "I work in marketing and public relations for a living and I excel at it. I've been noticing some things around here, many things, actually, that you could be doing better. The place is lovely, Luke, but it needs sprucing up. You've got to do more advertising, too. I probably wouldn't have known about it if my friend hadn't told me, and she knew about it because it's her job to find hidden gems—key word hidden."

She paused for a breath and Luke worked to control his own shaky breath, as anger coursed through his bloodstream.

Who does she think she is?

"I think my family—" he emphasized *family* "—ranch is

doing just fine, and if it wasn't, it certainly wouldn't be up to you, a guest from the city, to fix things."

Bella looked slightly taken aback, but only slightly. Suddenly, Luke could picture her in business meetings, probably pushing her ideas on others.

"But showing things to their full advantage is what I do," she explained in a patient kind of way, which somehow infuriated him even more.

But, Luke quickly realized, he had to do something with that. He couldn't unleash his anger and dismay—or his secret fear that she might be right about the ranch—on anyone, especially not a guest.

He was relieved when he saw Alison coming down a path then cutting across the field headed in their direction.

When she was within calling distance, Alison gave her message with all the enthusiasm of a delivery person on a rainy day.

"Grandma wants you up at the house."

"Did she say why?" Luke asked, his forehead creasing into a frown, though he was actually relieved to get away from the conversation that Bella had started.

Alison glared at Lily, who had stopped, Hooligan halting alongside her.

"I don't know why you're letting her think Hooligan likes her," Alison sneered.

"Did Grandma say why she needs me at the house?" Luke repeated the question. He wasn't going to bring further attention to Alison's comment.

"No, and I didn't appreciate being told to come all the way out here to tell you. That's all I know."

Luke was silent, pondering how to best deal with the situation. He couldn't leave Bella and Lily alone with the horse, and he wasn't keen on asking someone else to step in.

He hadn't liked seeing Cal hanging around their cabin that morning. He didn't appreciate Bella's unwanted input but he wasn't about to leave her or Lily in the hands of someone like Cal.

"I thought you'd like a break, Uncle Luke," Alison said, putting her hands on her hips and a slight mocking emphasis on *uncle*. "Since you don't really like the horses."

First, Bella basically telling him that the ranch was a failure and now Alison's comments.

It really wasn't his day.

Chapter Five

Luke Duffy was tall enough that Bella, who was tall herself, had to tilt her chin up slightly when she talked to him. His shoulders filled out his T-shirt in a pleasing way. He had a strong jaw, often wore a determined expression and was, all in all, what one might imagine when dreaming up a handsome rancher.

Even though, after that night, she was never going to dream of a handsome rancher or anyone else.

Still, seeing the chagrin on Luke's face, like a boy caught smuggling home a bad report card, combined with the wound in his eyes caused a surge of protectiveness that rivaled what she experienced with Lily to surge through her.

She wasn't used to remembering that men could need protection too. There were circumstances and people that could wound them.

The realization sat uneasily on her shoulders and she wasn't sure what she wanted to do with it.

"You don't even like horses?" Bella repeated Alison's words while she hovered with a watchful expression.

Lily was watching too. She hung on to Hooligan's reins like she'd been born to do it. The horse even rested his large head on her shoulder, a sure sign of trust and confidence.

"I like them just fine," Luke said, biting off the words. "As

I've been reminding everyone, they are unpredictable animals and need to be treated with respect."

"Mr. Duffy?" Lily addressed him directly, something she rarely did with people she didn't know well. "You had a bad experience with a horse, didn't you?"

Bella watched a myriad of expressions cross Luke's face, but she was very sure of one thing: Lily had guessed correctly. Her shy daughter had a knack for doing that. People often made the mistake of thinking that because Lily didn't want attention on her it meant that she wasn't paying attention.

There was a long moment of silence before Luke answered, and Bella half expected him to deny it. But then he said, "I'll tell you about it sometime."

He directed his next words to Bella: "But that doesn't mean that I don't believe in what we're doing here, or what these horses are capable of. I may be learning as I go, but if I didn't think this would end well for all of us, I wouldn't be doing it."

Bella lifted her chin and studied his eyes. Satisfied by what she saw there, she gave one brief nod.

Still, she intended to keep her eyes and ears wide open. No matter how happy Lily was with Hoolie, if anything struck her wrong, or as being less than what the ranch had promised, they were out of here.

"Grandma is still waiting," Alison said sharply, and Bella spotted a flare of jealousy in her eyes.

She doesn't like her uncle getting along with us, especially not with Lily.

She guessed that Alison's obnoxious attitude hid insecurity. Whatever it was her parents were doing, they'd excluded her from it, and that had to hurt.

"That's a pretty color on you," Bella said, indicating the top Alison wore. Its swirls of greens and blues reminded her of ocean waves and brought out the girl's eyes.

Luke worked his jaw, sighing.

"I'm sorry," he said after a pause. "We'll have to take Hooligan back to the barn for now. I promise this won't happen again, and I'll make the time up to you."

"You shouldn't make promises you can't keep, Luke," Alison said. Before anyone could react, she was off, running across the field.

Luke stroked his chin and looked like there were about a hundred things he wanted to say.

"Thank you for being nice to her" was what came out. "I know she isn't easy to deal with."

"She's young," Bella said mildly. "I'm guessing this isn't where she would have chosen to spend her summer."

She wasn't going to push for more details. It didn't concern her other than how it might impact Lily and their time here. Or, at least, that was what she would tell herself.

"I would want the same for Lily," she added. "I mean, for someone to understand that, even on her worst days, she's worth loving."

"Her parents are traveling," Luke said, answering the question she hadn't wanted to ask. "They're working on their marriage." The latter words were seasoned with a tang of bitterness. He abruptly stopped talking and lengthened his stride to catch up with Lily and Hooligan as they were reaching the barn, leaving Bella to speculate on his reaction to their travels…and also what Alison had meant about him not making promises he couldn't keep.

When he exited the barn, he appeared calmer, but clearly there was a lot going on with this family.

It was not only a big part of Bella's profession but also inherent to her personality to want to first figure out what was wrong and then try to fix it, but she could not allow herself to forget what this time on the ranch was supposed to do for Lily and her.

She would need to keep reminding herself not to be taken in by Luke Duffy's mixture of strength and vulnerability.

"I'll make sure this doesn't take long," Luke said, as they walked back up toward the house.

The outdoor surroundings somewhat soothed Bella's questioning mind. The air smelled so fresh, the greenery was abundant and the fields beckoned for adventure.

"I hope things are okay," Bella said.

"With my mother, it could be anything," Luke said, then he shook his head. "I don't mean that the way it sounded. She's had a rough time since my father passed."

"I'm so sorry," Bella said. "It's hard to lose someone."

"Are your parents…?" Luke looked down at her.

"Both alive and enjoying life in a retirement community."

He nodded, "Ahh."

"But I have lost people I was close to," Bella added, thinking of when her paternal grandmother died. They had shared a love for God and both liked to plan and make lists. She was the one person whom she'd come the closest to telling the truth about Lily's father.

They neared the house.

"I'm really sorry again for the interruption," Luke said. "I… I don't think my mother realized that I would be the one helping Lily with the horses. She just seems to feel completely helpless. My dad was a real take-charge kind of guy, she never had to do much but support him, and I think it's overwhelming for her to have decisions to make, so she always needs me for something."

He mussed his hair with an agitated hand.

"I want to be there for her, but I have other responsibilities too. I just pray I can do it all."

Lily, who had been quiet, seeming unabsorbed in the conversation to that point, jerked her head up.

"If you can't teach me with the horses, I don't want that Cal."

Sometimes Bella had to remind even herself that her daughter was always paying attention, even when it didn't appear that way.

"Cal won't be working with you," Luke said with a calm voice but fierce eyes.

When they got inside, Nora was at the kitchen table, looking like a lost child.

"Would you like to go to the library again?" Luke offered Bella and Lily

Lily gave a half nod, unable to hide her disappointment at the interruption to her plans.

Bella hesitated, not knowing what she should do. What she really wanted was to sit down with Luke and his mother and figure out once and for all whether it was worth staying or not.

On the other hand, whenever she was faced with a tough situation, she had never been able to resist finding out if there was anything she could do to fix it.

Bella had followed her daughter to the library, but Luke sensed her reluctance to do so. He didn't know how he felt about that. His attractive guest was hard to read. He had caught moments where she was like a fragile fawn ready to flee. But also other moments when she seemed to want to dig in her heels and figure things out.

Except it wasn't her place to figure any of it out. That was his job. He had to figure out how to deal with his family issues and not lose a paying guest in the process.

"Where's Alison?" was Luke's first question to his mother after their guests departed. "Did she come back up here?"

"I think she's in her room," his mother said with the vagueness that colored most of her interactions with Alison.

"What did you need me for, Mom?" Luke asked, willing himself to be patient, but unable to restrain himself from adding, "I was just starting a therapy horse session with our guests, and you know we're counting on that for extra income."

"I want to start going through Sly's cabinets, the ones with all the business files.

Why today? Luke wanted to ask. The cabinets had been sitting in Sly's office since he passed, and any time he or Brett mentioned purging them, their mother wanted no part of it.

"Brett and I will be able to help you with that when he's back," he said. His older brother wouldn't want him making decisions about their father's papers without him, nor did he feel equipped to do so.

His mother's shoulders drooped. "I was hoping to get a start on it today."

"Is another month or two going to make a difference now, Mom? What brought this about?"

"Dan Cooper said that it's a good idea to make sure all the documents are in order before a sale."

"I'm sure he did." Luke was taut with apprehension. "Look, Mom, I don't want you discussing anything about Dad's papers or anything about the sale of the ranch with anyone without me around, okay?"

In his mind, he was already reaching out to their lawyer.

His mother's eyes sparked, showing a remnant of spunk and reminding Luke that she had once been a full partner to his father.

Now, as she looked at him with the sternness he remembered from childhood, Luke didn't want to make the mistake of underestimating her.

"This is still my ranch, Luke," she said. "It's still my name on the deed and in Sly's will. I think I'm entitled to talk to who I want about it."

"Mom," Luke said, mustering all of his willpower not to let his agitation show in his voice. "Dad would not have approved of selling the ranch to the Coopers."

He silently added that Sly Duffy, who had lived and breathed the ranching life like the horses and the sky and land all combined to make up his DNA, would not have wanted the ranch sold to anyone under any circumstances.

So why did he make the decisions that he did near the end? Lord, will I ever be able to turn things around?

"Don't you remember all those rodeos when they were questioned for their methods?" he persisted. "They've never been above board. Dad knew that, and I'm sure he'd want you to remember that too."

His mother's fierce expression collapsed into sadness and confusion again.

"I just don't know what do," she almost whispered, directing the words to her teacup. "This ranch is draining money, and I don't know what to do to fix it, and right now the Coopers are the only ones making any kind of an offer."

"I'll fix it, Mom," Luke promised with a certainty he didn't feel. "I'll figure out a way to do it. I promise."

And, if Dad is looking down on us, maybe he'll finally be proud of me.

"I was telling Luke that I think I can help," Bella's voice said.

"And I was telling her that we don't need her help," Luke responded.

She stood in the doorway, and he wondered how long she'd been standing there eavesdropping on his discussion with his mother on their family problems.

"I didn't mean to eavesdrop," Bella answered the silent question. "I was coming in to get a glass of water for Lily…"

Her voice trailed off as her eyes flitted in Luke's direction then away like cautious birds.

Luke watched his mother recover her company manners.

Nora Duffy still had moments of remembering the woman she had been when she knew she was backing a man to be reckoned with, but her common state these days was one of grief, being overwhelmed and fear of the future.

Luke didn't blame her, not one bit.

But here she was, rising with an impressively convincing smile on her face, offering Bella a seat at their family table and instructing Luke to get a glass of water for Lily.

As Luke retrieved the water pitcher out of the fridge, Bella crossed the kitchen to him and stood beside him.

"I'd like to talk to you," she said quietly.

On some level, he couldn't help considering what she had said about her expertise and allowed himself to briefly wonder if she really could help. But he had no desire to talk to her or to hear her litany of all the ways his family home was a failure.

The night before, he'd sent a text to Brett:

Hey, hope things going well but could really use you here.

It hadn't been long before the unsatisfactory reply came.

Sorry, bro, dealing with my marriage here. I'm sure you can manage, can't you?

The two-word question could be perceived to have been tossed unthinkingly at the end of the text. But Brett was Sly's son through and through, more than Luke had ever been, and he knew that his older brother really was questioning what he was capable of.

Still, he wasn't coming back to the ranch or offering any words of wisdom.

Bella's request still lingered in the air.

"What do you want to talk about?" he asked Bella through tightened lips.

"What I was telling you before. I have some ideas for your ranch. What you could do here. I have headed up numerous campaigns that have brought client's businesses to the forefront, using social media and other proven methods. I'm sure I could do the same for you."

He wanted to ask her if she was joking. She'd come here as a guest just a couple of days ago; she'd expressed more than once that she wasn't sure if they were staying because things weren't quite what she'd expected. And now she wouldn't drop this inane idea of helping them.

He shook his head but didn't realize that he'd actually done, so Bella said, "I know how this must sound but, like I said, I do this kind of thing for a living and I do it well."

"But you're not a rancher," Luke said flatly. "Unless you've been raised that way, I doubt you can help."

He got a glass out of the cupboard, poured the water and handed it to her. "For Lily," he said, indicating it was the end of the conversation.

Bella thinned her own lips and took the glass from him. He had a split-second flash of one of those overly dramatic scenes in a movie when an unhappy heroine flings water in the hero's face.

It almost made him laugh…almost.

They studied each other, each trying to read the other's face like they were written in a foreign tongue.

"Bella, dear," Luke's mother spoke up, snapping the moment into pieces. "After you take the water to your little girl, can you come back here please? I'd like to hear more about what you have to say."

"About what, Mom?" His tone, even to his own ears, conveyed the question, *What could she possibly have to say that you'd need or want to hear?*

"Weren't you listening, Luke? Bella said she could help us with the ranch."

Exasperation snaked through Luke with fangs at the ready.

But then a thought occurred to him. If his mother wanted to hear what Bella had to say, and *if,* by some off chance, what she had to say held any real value, then maybe talk of selling the ranch could be postponed, at least for a little while.

He turned to Bella with his best "Howdy, ma'am" grin.

"Yes, please come back here. I'd love to hear what you have to say."

Chapter Six

Why did I say anything? Bella questioned herself as she returned to the library with Lily's glass of water.

The expression on Luke's face clearly said that he wondered the same thing. She wanted to think she didn't care what he thought, but—without knowing exactly why—she did. At least, she didn't want to be the person to pile more stress onto a plate that was already full to overflowing.

That was why she *had* said something, Bella reasoned with herself. She had always seen challenges as opportunities; it was what made her so good at her job.

Her mind churned, already planning ahead. If she could give Luke and Nora ideas for what would really make this place shine, she would not only have the satisfaction of a job well-done, but she could also ensure that Lily's time here would be everything it needed to be.

It was also something she could put on her resume. Maybe New Hope Ranch would even become a new client of theirs… and maybe then Felicity would let the whole Jeb Martin issue go.

Maybe…

"Took you long enough," Lily grumbled.

It wasn't her daughter's nature to be rude, Bella knew, but she was reacting to the disappointment of her first horse therapy session being interrupted.

"I'm sorry, Lily-pad." Bella handed her the water, which Lily promptly put on the table beside her without drinking it.

"How long is Luke going to be?" she asked. "He's taking me and Hoolie out again, isn't he?"

"I don't know how long, but I'm sure he will as soon as he can."

It was funny how she did know, Bella mused. It wasn't at all easy for her to trust men, after her past experience, but she tended to be perceptive about people in general, both naturally and as a skill she'd developed in her work, and she knew that Luke Duffy was a man who wanted to do—actually more than that—he was a man who was compelled to do what he promised.

"Actually, are you okay in here for a few more minutes?" she asked anxiously.

Lily's small face scrunched in suspicion. "Why?"

"The Duffys want to talk to me about a couple of things— just some things about being on the ranch."

Bella held her breath a little, hopeful that Lily wouldn't ask more questions. The last thing she needed her thinking was that her mother was turning this into a business trip.

I'm not, I'm really not.

"Are you going to keep reading *My Friend Flicka*?" Bella asked, as a way to ease past the other topic.

Lily shrugged.

"Tell Luke I'm waiting." She picked up the water then and took a big gulp.

"We'll be as fast as we can," Bella promised.

As she went back to the kitchen, the family pictures on the wall caught Bella out of the corner of her eye. When she had more time, she would stop and have a better look.

Her heart thudded a bit when she saw Luke and Nora waiting for her at the kitchen table, but she reminded herself that she had faced down more intimidating clients than these, not to mention her demanding boss.

"Take a seat," Luke said, in a manner that made her wonder for a moment if two-way mirrors were going to be involved.

"Would you like some tea?" Nora offered.

If this was going to be an interrogation, she would definitely be the good cop.

"A glass of water would be nice, actually." Bella's throat was a little dry from nervousness.

"Luke," Nora said, lifting her chin in the direction of the refrigerator.

"I can get it myself," Bella interjected. "Would anyone else like a glass?"

"No," Luke said. "Thank you."

How was it that three perfectly polite words could make her want to squirm with awkwardness?

"Is it okay if I talk first?" Luke said when Bella sat down. It wasn't really a question, she knew.

She took a sip of water, and it sounded loud in her own ears when she swallowed. "Of course."

Luke Duffy was a very handsome man, she noted, even with the stern expression that adorned his face. But why was she thinking of that? This was not the time to be noticing that. There wasn't a good time for her to notice that about any man.

"First of all," Luke said, "I want to apologize that you've inadvertently been party to conversations about some of the difficulties the ranch is having. We should not be having these conversations when there are guests around." Here he paused and sneaked a look in his mother's direction.

Nora toyed with her teaspoon and stubbornly refused to make eye contact.

He turned his attention back to Bella. She was a butterfly pinned under the intensity of his gaze.

"You are a guest here, and going forward, we both need to remember that. We certainly can't and don't expect you to solve problems you weren't meant to hear about in the first place. I need to do my part too to be a better host. What happened this morning will not happen again."

Again, Bella sensed that the latter words were for his mother's benefit.

"I hope this clears things up between us," Luke said, looking slightly softer since he'd had his say.

"May I speak now?"

Bella heard her business voice take over, felt her posture shift.

It was nothing she did purposely, but it was something that took over when she needed to make sure that her ideas weren't overlooked.

She could tell by the change in Luke's posture and his almost concealed intake of breath that he noticed the change as well.

"You may…" he said cautiously.

"First of all, I know that we are guests here, and I also know that your family's business is just that, your business. I'm not trying to poke my nose in where it doesn't belong to make your lives more difficult than they seem to be. I'm offering professional help. Marketing and public relations is what I do for a living, and I'm good at it, very good, in fact. I could give you references or show you websites of some of the accounts I've worked on."

She paused to take a breath, and Luke said, "Excuse me, but didn't you come here to help your daughter because you thought that working with the therapy horses would be good for her? I didn't realize you were trying to drum up business for yourself."

He didn't actually accuse her of being self-serving and a bad mother, but Bella stiffened under his censure.

I am a good mother. That's why I'm doing this.

Nora stopped stirring her tea, which she'd been doing absent-mindedly since putting a cube of sugar into it, and gently placed the spoon on the side of her plate. Within her politely neutral face, her eyes were avid with interest, waiting for Bella's response.

"I didn't come here with any other intention than to make sure that Lily has a good summer," Bella said, looking back and forth between Luke and his mother. "That's still my primary intention, but that isn't going to happen when you're dealing with problems here, is it?"

She didn't want or mean to be so blunt and almost wished she could inhale back her words when she saw the way Luke ducked his head like a schoolboy who had to tell his parents he'd failed another math test.

But, no, she couldn't let herself be soft. She had to keep hoping that she could make a difference in how their summer, and their future, would turn out.

And maybe she needed to prove to herself that she still had something to offer. Felicity's attitude was chipping away at her self-esteem.

Luke scratched his chin, his nails making a scraping sound against the bristle of new whiskers that sprouted there.

Either he was struggling with what to say next, Bella thought, or he was struggling to hold back from saying too much.

"You think you can help us, do you?" Nora asked.

"Not that we're saying that we need help," Luke quickly added.

"Yes, I'm sure I can," Bella answered.

"Why would you want to?" Luke persisted.

"Because I'm not the kind of person who can see something that needs fixing and not want to fix it," Bella said.

That was about as blunt as she could get.

Luke drummed his fingers on the table. His hands were strong, tanned and looked like they understood a good day's work.

But that strength of will failed to meet his eyes. Bella could tell that he knew that things were falling apart around him and he was like a hamster on a treadmill, running to catch up but not getting anywhere.

But in no way did that mean that she thought he was inadequate or incapable. There was something in him that was tied to the land here: something strong and loyal that ran deep.

A person might even be able to count on a man like that.

Bella mentally shook her head.

"You've been here for just a couple of days," Luke said, "and you not only think you've got our problems figured out, you think you've got a way to fix them?"

Behind his biting tone, Bella heard a faint whisper of someone who longed for an answer.

"I think so, yes," she replied. "I've only been here a couple of days, as you say. But already I see that you're pulled in too many different directions."

"You can't fix that."

"You're right," Bella agreed. She knew there was no more disarming a tactic than to agree with your opponent. Except Luke wasn't her opponent, not exactly.

What exactly is he?

"What I can do, though," she said with the attention of both Duffys on her, "is help you draw more attention to this place so you have more guests. More guests equals more money, and pretty soon you may find you can hire more help so that you aren't torn in so many directions. You can focus on the things that are important to you."

"But we have help, dear," Nora interjected. "Cal Wayman has been with the ranch for years."

At the mention of Cal's name, Luke caught Bella's eye and the distaste in his was plain.

I don't think he likes Cal.

"Cal isn't really suited for the direction I want the ranch to go in," Luke said, and for the first time in the conversation, Bella was sure he was giving full consideration to what she had to say.

"Okay, say I'm willing to concede that we need help drawing customers in," Luke continued, speaking slowly. "I still don't get how this is going to work with the reason you brought Lily here."

Bella took in a deep breath and sent up a prayer as she breathed it out.

Please let me be doing the right thing.

Because she never put herself in a position to spend more time around a man than she had to.

"I'm going to spend time with you while you teach Lily, and at the same time, I'll be observing, seeing what strengths are here and the best way to sell them."

Luke held her gaze for a long, thoughtful moment; his eyes were blue beacons, drawing her in.

Bella inwardly pulled back.

He didn't take his eyes off her but directed his next words to Nora.

"Mom, if we give this a try, will you stop talking to the Coopers or anyone else about a sale?"

"I suppose," Nora fretted. "But there's still so much to consider."

Luke gave one slow nod. "We'll figure it out."

He extended his hand and said, "Okay, Bella, let's see how this goes."

He closed his strong, warm hand around hers, and they shook on it.

Bella imagined that Luke's handshake was conveying a message to her. *I'm deciding to trust you.*

She didn't want to disappoint him…almost as much as she didn't want to disappoint herself.

What have I just agreed to, Lord?

After they'd shook hands, Bella had wanted to get back to Lily, saying something about being gone longer than she'd intended.

Now, he remained in the kitchen with his mother's accusing eyes on him.

"I hope you know what you're doing, Lucas."

"You were the one who wanted to hear what she had to say," he reminded her.

"I was curious, yes," his mother agreed. "I don't want anything to get in the way of selling this place."

This place? When did she start calling our home this place?

Luke stayed silent, afraid if he spoke too quickly, his voice would betray the painful emotions that ripped through him.

He took in the paint chips in the deep, woodsy brown of the walls, saw that the flowered curtains at the kitchen window looked a bit frayed and studied the map of scuff marks on the kitchen-floor hardwood that told countless stories of their comings and goings.

Even with paint chips, frayed curtains and scuffed floors, this kitchen—this whole house—told the story of their lives.

He wasn't going to sell those memories, especially not to people like the Coopers.

"Do you really want to sell, Mom?" he asked. "Think of

everything this house has meant to you, to our family." He hated to play the Sly card but had to add, "Do you think it's what Dad would have wanted?"

The fierce light in his mother's eyes faded to a perplexed glimmer.

"I spent our whole marriage thinking I knew what your father wanted," she said. "But that all changed when I found out he'd made all those bad investments before he passed. Now, all I know is that we can't afford this place, and the sooner it's off our hands, the sooner we'll be able to get on with life."

"But maybe Bella's ideas will help," Luke said, letting himself consider for the first time that maybe they really could.

She was definitely determined, he could say that much for her. He did admire her grit…when it wasn't driving him around the bend.

"You did promise you'd hold off, Mom," he reminded his mother.

"I didn't feel like I had much of a choice," His mother sniffed. She got up to add hot water to her teacup.

"Mom," Luke said, "please believe me, I'm so sorry for the way things have gone down. I don't believe that you really want to sell New Hope, despite what you say, so I'm doing my best to come up with a solution."

"I think you'd better get back to work, Luke."

Well, at least it wasn't *Lucas* anymore.

He realized that they hadn't returned to the subject of going through Sly's papers, but that was probably best for now.

He found Bella and Lily in the library, sitting on the horsehair loveseat, their heads bent together over an old issue of a women's magazine.

"Why don't you have an apron like that, Mom?" Lily quipped in a dry tone. "Hey, I just got a great idea for next Mother's Day!"

"You don't think I'd totally rock that apron?" Bella jumped up and struck a couple of poses.

"Eww, Mom, no one says things like *totally rock* anymore." But Lily was laughing along with her mother.

Luke lingered in the doorway, not announcing his presence. He felt the corners of his mouth lifting into a smile. He didn't mean to spy on them, but he couldn't remember the last time pure enjoyment tapped at the barricade of constant worry and regret that surrounded him.

He also couldn't help being intrigued to witness this goofy side of Bella. She had barriers of her own, he knew. He just didn't know why.

"How about a hairnet to go with that apron?" Bella said, twisting her hair up in a knot with one hand and placing the other hand on her hip while she strutted. "Maybe that could be in my Christmas stocking."

Lily spotted him then. "Uhh, Mom…"

"What?" Bella had her back to him, but then did her best fashion runway spin and saw him too.

She flushed and let her hair tumble down. Luke admired its sand and caramel shades.

Such a pretty color…

"We were just, umm…"

"Having a laugh," Luke said. "That's great. We could use more of that around here. Anyway," he addressed Lily, who appeared to be properly mortified by someone else witnessing her mother's silly behavior, "are you ready to go see Hooligan again?"

"Definitely," Lily cheered.

"Yes, that sounds great," Bella added, reminding him with a look what they had shook on in the kitchen.

"Your mom's going to come too," Luke said.

"I guess she thinks you might hurt yourself," Alison drawled, standing behind Luke.

Despite her sarcastic attitude, he couldn't help wishing that she'd been part of the silly fun over the aprons and hair nets. She probably didn't even know herself how much she needed to cut loose and let herself be a kid.

The way Lily drew back into herself when she heard Alison's voice was like watching a hibiscus close up its blooms at the end of the day.

Luke watched Bella send Lily a brief look that conveyed comfort and encouragement and most of all said *Be strong. You can do this.*

It troubled him. His niece was a troubled girl, not a monster.

"Why don't you come too, Alison?" Bella suggested, bringing out the tone that had set Luke back a few paces in the kitchen.

"It sounds like you know a lot about horses," Bella continued. "It would be great if you could share some of the knowledge."

A challenge had unmistakably been made.

Luke choked back a laugh when he saw the look on Alison's face. She only let her disinterested expression drop for a second, but he caught it and that was enough.

Behind her mother, though, Lily's shoulders were hunched, and she was grimacing so hard it threatened to leave permanent lines in her forehead.

Bella noticed too and put her arm around the girl's slender shoulders, whispering something in her ear that relaxed some of the tension in her face.

Alison made a disgusted noise, and Luke turned to scold her. But something in her eyes stopped him, and he was reminded that, despite what her attitude conveyed, she was still just a young girl whose parents had left her here.

"You should come, Alley-cat," he encouraged, surprising himself with the childhood nickname that had sprung suddenly to his mind.

A startled flicker in her eyes showed that she was surprised too.

Dear Lord, please help me to be a better uncle to her, to pay more attention to what's really happening here.

"Girls, will you give me a minute to talk to Lily's mom?" he asked.

Bella nodded at Lily, who reluctantly went to stand out in the hallway. She turned her back to Alison, while Alison tugged at one of the oversize gold-hoop earrings she wore.

"I appreciate that you're trying to be understanding to Alison," Luke said.

"I am trying, but I don't want anything to ruin Lily's experience either."

"I'm not going to let that happen," Luke replied. "Believe me, I know how Alison comes across, but sometimes I look at her and I remember her as a little girl and how she used to love to run around here, climbing trees and feeding the horses and helping my mother in the kitchen. She wasn't always like this. I think… I think that being left here by her parents while they travel is bothering her more than she wants to say."

As Bella listened, sympathy poured into her blue eyes.

"Don't you think sometimes," Luke mused, "that the more people need others, the more they might tend to push them away?"

The sympathy changed to something else, something slightly guarded.

"Sometimes there are reasons not to let people get too close," Bella said, almost as if to herself.

Luke found himself holding his breath, waiting to hear if she would reveal more. It was like approaching a skittish animal: move too fast or assume too much, and she would be gone.

But then she blinked and said in a brisk tone, "I'm sorry, I get defensive of Lily and let myself forget sometimes that I'm the adult in the situation. Of course, Alison is welcome to do whatever she wants to do. This is your ranch. She's your niece."

"She probably doesn't even want to come," Luke conceded. "She pretty much tries to avoid her grandma and me at all costs."

Bella furrowed her brow. "What does she do all day? Is she just up in her room most of the time? Do you know what she does there?"

Luke shifted uncomfortably and cleared his throat, trying to think of a way to justify that he'd had too much on his mind to pay much attention.

"I guess I haven't thought about it much," he mumbled.

Bella chewed her lower lip thoughtfully.

Luke waited for the lecture to commence, but instead her smile was more sympathetic than he would have expected when she said, "It's not easy being a single parent, is it?"

He wasn't really a single parent, but she was letting him know that she understood the challenges he faced.

He nodded and gave her a half smile, still trying to puzzle out the various pieces of this woman.

The conversation stirred curiosity about Bella's circumstances.

"Is Lily's father…?" he began.

"Not in the picture." She cut him off, any softness gone and replaced by the sharp edges that kept others away.

Something happened to her.

"We shouldn't keep the girls waiting any longer," Bella said, all briskness again. She tapped the side of her cheek with one finger. "Alison seems like the type who likes to have her opinions heard."

Luke nodded, "I think that's fair to say."

"Maybe she can help me notice things about the ranch, point them out, let me know what she thinks."

"Like a consultant?" Luke wondered where she was going with this.

"Like someone who's being asked to get involved because she matters," Bella said. "We'll all be together, but you'll be focused on Lily and the horses, which is what Lily needs. But I thought that if Alison knew she had a role to play too, it might help."

Once again, Luke thought he saw a glimmer of the vulnerability that Bella hid behind the business-like exterior she presented.

I'll never figure her out.

He reminded himself that he didn't have to. She was a guest—granted, a guest who thought she could save their ranch—and he was their host, who wanted only to live up to their expectations…and not have them worry about a ranch that needed saving.

Chapter Seven

Bella didn't honestly expect Alison to want to have anything to do with them. She couldn't even imagine the clearly unhappy teenager traipsing around the ranch with her.

But her heart stirred with empathy, knowing that she could probably write the book on hiding hurt behind a tough exterior.

Regardless of how Alison reacted, though, there was no way Bella was going to linger in any conversation about Lily's father.

Thankfully, Luke hadn't persisted or even seemed to react to her terse response. But still, her insides churned uneasily. She hoped that this summer would be a reprieve from Lily's increasing demands to know more about her father. But dread like a chilly drizzle washed over Bella as she knew that she wouldn't be able to escape the questions forever.

"I'm kind of surprised they didn't bolt," Luke said out of the side of his mouth when they found Lily and Alison still lingering in the hallway, studiously ignoring each other.

The way he said it made Bella suspect there was a dry sense of humor lingering beneath the surface of this man who had so much to deal with.

"How'd you like to help me out today, Alison?" she asked.

For a few seconds, she and Lily did their mother-daughter, communicate-without-words thing, with Lily's eyes asking what was going on and Bella's answering that she would explain later.

A wary expression crossed Alison's face as she asked, "With what?"

"Well, I'm in marketing and public relations," Bella explained. "And it's one of the facets of my work that I'm always looking at how places look and how they're run and what I can do to help bring out the best in them so that everyone else can see how great they are too."

"Okaaay," Alison drawled out the word, scratching her nose.

"You obviously care a lot about this place and know far more about it than I do," Bella continued. "I was hoping you could help me make sure I don't miss anything."

"Me?" Alison said, her eyes narrowed in suspicion. "You want help from me?"

"If you've got the time, I would really appreciate it."

Alison gave Luke a look that asked if he had put Bella up to this.

"Come on, Al," he urged. "It's better than sitting up in your room, right?"

Alison folded her arms and put out her lower lip, and for a moment, Bella was afraid that the words meant to motivate her into action would backfire.

But then she breathed out and said, "Okay, I guess."

Luke caught Bella's eye and gave her a slight nod, which she returned.

Though she never let herself think about it, she imagined this was how parents working together over a difficult child might feel.

As they walked to the barn, Bella could tell that Lily was hanging back, wanting to talk to her out of earshot of the others.

"Why are you asking for *her* help?" she demanded in a hissing whisper.

"Because she needs something productive and positive to do," Bella said, being as honest as she could be. "Luke is going to be busy with you and the horses, so I thought it would be nice if I offered to have Alison hang out with me."

"But she's horrible," Lily protested, scrunching up her face like she smelled something bad. Anxiety leapt into her eyes. "If she's around, it's going to ruin my whole summer."

"I would never let that happen," Bella promised, but doubt clawed at her gut as she wondered if she could live up to that promise.

Lily was a mature, observant girl, though, and often being as straightforward with her as possible was the best way to go.

"Have you noticed we're the only guests here?" Bella began.

Lily hesitated then nodded. "Well, yes, but I just thought it's because it's still early in the summer."

"It's not that early," Bella commented. "A place like this, doing what it says it wants to do, should be all booked up by now. Luke has too much to do," she continued explaining, "and I was afraid that if I didn't find some way to help him then you really wouldn't have the kind of summer you want with the horses. Does that make sense?"

"You're putting up with Alison so I don't have to," Lily said dryly.

Bella barked out a laugh—her shy daughter's astute and sometimes cutting observations always caught her off guard—causing the two in front of them to turn around. Alison frowned, but Luke looked curious and a bit wistful, like he wished he was in on the joke.

I'm going to have to be careful not to let myself get soft toward this man.

"I guess you could say that," Bella chuckled. "I want Luke

to be able to focus as much of his time on you as possible, so I told him that I would see what I could do to help."

Lily stopped walking and tilted her chin up to study her mother's face.

"You want to go all PR on this ranch, don't you?" she asked in a slightly accusing way.

Many excuses she could give spun through Bella's mind, but there was only one answer: it was for the same reason she made all of her choices.

"I'm doing it for you. I want to make sure you have the best time you can have."

It was the truth, she reasoned with herself, watching Lily lead Hooligan out of the barn. If this ended up being the answer to her work dilemma as well, it would just help her believe more deeply that God had a plan.

Alison stood off to one side, her head tilted at a critical angle, watching Lily.

Bella gritted her teeth, reminding herself that there was nothing to interfere with, at least not yet. Then her attention was drawn to Luke, who stood with his head down, his muscular chest moving with deep breaths in and out.

Was he praying?

Bella remembered that he'd promised Lily he would tell her a story about an experience he'd had with horses. The implication was that it hadn't been a pleasant one. Yet, there he was, standing in the field with Lily and Hooligan, making an effort so that his guests wouldn't be disappointed.

Curiosity sparked in Bella, urging her to be present when Luke told his story.

But no, sharing confidences was usually intended to be reciprocal. If he shared personal things with her, he might well expect her to open up in return, and she couldn't risk that.

There was no way she was letting things get personal because it might lead to more curiosity about Lily's father.

Bella frowned thinking of how she was running into men who reminded her of *him* far too often: first Jed through her work and here Cal Wayman.

With shiver-inducing timing, the sun slipped momentarily behind a cloud, and the day was suddenly chilled and bleak.

Just breathe. Focus on something that comforts you and helps you feel safe.

Bella silently repeated to herself the words that she often said to Lily when her daughter was having an especially hard time in certain situations.

She couldn't hear what Luke was saying, but she could see by his nod and smile that he was offering encouragement to Lily. Lily took Hoolie's reins and led him a few steps away, then she stopped. The horse stopped too and rested his head on Lily's shoulder.

Lily grinned widely, and Luke walked over to her and gave her a high five.

He said something else to Lily, and she nodded and led Hooligan in another direction while he watched them.

He looked at home in his surroundings in a way that Bella knew few people truly did. The way he loved this land showed in his attentive expression, the way he took in deep breaths of air, the way, when he moved toward the girl and the horse again, his boots trod the land both like he trusted it to hold him and like he respected it.

Comfortable... Safe.

Was she believing that a man could hold those qualities?

"Did you really want my help?" Alison said with a fake innocence. "Or did you just drag me out here so you could stare at Luke?"

"Uncle Luke," Bella said automatically and realized that the same words were spoken simultaneously by the man himself.

Does that mean he heard what Alison said?

Alison raised her arms with a don't-gang-up-on-me look. "How's it going out there, *Uncle* Luke? It looks like she's got leading the horse around down pat." Her voice dripped with sarcastic praise.

Usually, Bella might have stepped in with some sort of retort, but she'd decided earlier that she had to be the adult, and besides, Lily would never grow in confidence if she kept stepping into situations instead of letting her work things out.

More than that, though, in this particular moment, she was happy for the distraction and for a moment to regroup.

She *had* been staring at Luke, and she had no idea why, at least no idea that she was willing to admit.

"What would you be doing with Hooligan if you were working with him?" Bella asked when she was sure her musings over her uncharacteristic behavior wouldn't show on her face.

She was well practiced at keeping a neutral expression around hard-to-please clients, but Alison gave the impression that she could see right through her.

"What difference does it make?" The teenager shrugged and pushed her pretty auburn hair behind her ears to reveal tiny silver cross earrings.

Was she a Christian? Bella wondered. She knew that all kinds of people were drawn to Jesus, even surly teenagers.

"I'm not working with him," Alison continued, "so what I think doesn't matter much."

"But you might have some good ideas that your uncle could put to use in getting more people interested in coming here."

Alison looked around. "It is kinda pathetic, isn't it?"

"Well, I wouldn't go that far…"

"Lily, watch out!" Luke's cautioning shout startled Bella,

and she turned, just in time to see her daughter slip and land flat on her back in a muddy spot on the field.

At least she hoped it was just mud.

She held her breath, arguing with herself about whether she should bolt over to Lily or not. Her daughter could be hurt, in which case Bella should go to her. Chances were, though, that it was her pride that was hurt more than anything, in which case, it was better to stay put and not make things worse.

Then a glorious sound lilted into the air. It was Lily laughing.

It had been so long since she'd heard her daughter's delightful giggle that Bella had almost forgotten how uplifting it was and how it could instantly change the mood of a room.

Or, in this case, a field.

Alison stared at the prone, giggling girl for a few seconds then her mouth quirked into a small smile.

She strode across the field toward Lily. Bella saw Luke watching, his face reflecting her own question about what was going to happen next.

Alison stopped, held out her hand and said, "If you aren't the goofiest kid." But she said it with a smile that softened the words, a smile that said that Lily was more of a trooper than she'd expected.

Lily reached out her hand, and Alison pulled her to her feet.

"Come on," the older girl said, as casually as if they'd been hanging out the entire time. "I'll show you how Hooligan likes to have his ears scratched."

The girls sauntered together to the horse, Lily oblivious to her muddy clothes.

Luke came up alongside Bella. He smelled of clean sweat and somehow of the wind and the trees.

"After seeing that," he murmured, "maybe I'm ready to believe that God still has plans for this place."

Bella nodded and swallowed, suddenly a bit afraid to look at him.

She would be happy if Lily and Alison could bond—it would make the summer go a lot more smoothly—but she didn't like the idea that it might bond her to Luke.

Bella and Lily, still their only guests, had been at New Hope for two weeks.

Luke was letting Lily set the pace on how much she wanted to do with Hoolie, and so far, she remained content grooming him, leading him around, giving him treats and chatting with him.

All of that suited him fine. It was restful to have one part of his day that was predictable.

His mother sometimes made a halfhearted effort to be the matriarch she'd been when Sly was alive, full of vigor and firm ideas about things, but she could never quite pull it off. His brother and sister-in-law remained on their travels, despite Luke's efforts to lure Brett home.

Alison couldn't believe that Lily didn't want to ride, and Luke had to remind her that the purpose of therapy horses was whatever worked best for the person interacting with them.

Certainly the friendship that had unexpectedly blossomed between Lily and Alison was a blessing, as it was a needed distraction for Alison, who must—though she never said it out loud—be wondering just how long her parents were going to act like they were childless honeymooners.

He had been worried at first that the relationship was going to be a painfully lopsided affair, with Alison calling all the shots. But it didn't take long for him to realize that Lily could hold her own.

This was something he realized he should have known, knowing her mother.

Bella also brought a fair degree of unpredictably into his days, but instead of making him want to burrow his stress headache into his hands, the things he couldn't figure out about her made something inside of him spark. He wasn't ready to catch fire, but still a spark was a whole lot more than he'd felt for a very long time.

It was too bad the timing couldn't have been more wrong.

Early Wednesday morning, Luke was woken up even earlier than his usual crack-of-dawn inner alarm clock by a cacophony of thunder and lightning.

He got out of bed, opened the drapes at his bedroom window and stood for a moment watching torrents of rain pour down while the prairie sky went bright then dark then bright again in a chaotic light show and thunder boomed, shaking the earth.

Lord, sometimes I forget Your power.

He had always loved a good storm, so much so that it took him a few minutes more to remember what his responsibilities were.

Luke sighed as he turned reluctantly from the window to prepare himself, mentally and physically, to go outside.

Although the horses were sheltered in the barn, he would need to check on their emotional state and wasn't too keen on finding them riled up. He also wondered how the rest of the household was doing.

If his mother wasn't sleeping, it would be her own thoughts keeping her awake. She had weathered—no pun intended— many storms alongside Sly, and the threat of weather wasn't the enemy that her own worries were to her.

Alison would never admit it if she was afraid, Luke thought, which left their guests to wonder about. But he wasn't going to check on them. That would be overstepping his boundaries as a host. If they needed anything, he was sure they would track him down.

But then, his thoughts continued to trouble him. Should he check on the horses, or should he wait a bit to see if the guests did need something? The guest cabin was well-built and secure, but still, what if the power went out while he was at the stables?

Don't be stupid. Bella is perfectly capable without you.

She was clearly intelligent, competent, fiercely protective of Lily—though he sensed she was trying to reel that in a bit—and it was obvious that she wanted to count on him for as little as possible, other than fulfilling his role in her summer plans, which was to teach Lily about the horses.

So why did he continue to think that there was something vulnerable in her? That she was someone who could use far more support and understanding than she would ever admit she needed?

Well, it was none of his business, and reading women wasn't really his top-level skill. That was proven by his being blissfully unaware that Gwen had transferred her affections to his brother until it became so blatantly obvious that it could no longer be ignored.

No, he had too much to do, too much to try to juggle in the present without limping after long-ago trails from the past.

Just as Luke turned to enter the hallway where his jacket and muck boots were, lightning flashed, causing a spotlight on Bella, who was coming in the side door.

She was dressed in navy sweatpants and a red rain jacket and clutched an umbrella that sported dancing mushrooms, but still rain cascaded off of her.

"What's wrong?" Luke asked, getting a grip on himself. "Is it the storm? Is your power out? Is Lily okay?"

He saw the corners of her mouth lift slightly at the tirade of questions, and he ordered himself to stop babbling.

"Lily is dead to the world," Bella said. "And, if she wasn't, she'd probably be looking out the window, watching the show. Being with people can make her nervous, but things like storms never do."

"Interesting," Luke said. "So, you're out getting soaked because…?"

Bella gave an embarrassed little shrug. "Because I couldn't sleep, and I was going to sneak in and find something to read and maybe grab a cup of tea. I wasn't expecting to run into anyone."

"You don't have anything to read in your cabin?"

Bud, you are killing it with the brilliant questions.

"No," she said, giving him a look. "But I'll make sure to rectify that for the future.

"I'm interrupting something," she added. "I'll get out of your way."

"I was going out to check on the horses," Luke acknowledged.

"Do you want company?"

The look on Bella's face reflected her own surprise at the offer and echoed how startled he was. But she let the offer stand.

"I don't want you getting soaked," Luke said automatically, then they both laughed as she spread her arms and looked down at herself, giving an exaggerated "Ahem!"

"Thanks for the offer," he said. "But I couldn't ask you to do that."

"You didn't ask, I offered."

Luke wasn't sure what to make of the offer, but after another moment of hesitation, he said, "At least let's take a decent umbrella. Yours looks like it's mostly for show."

"What?" Bella put on a fake pout. "You don't like dancing mushrooms?"

"No, I prefer them quiet and in my omelette."

The rain and wind had let up a bit by the time they stepped outside. Luke couldn't help enjoying the sensation of her closeness as they shared the umbrella.

A thought jumped into this mind: "What if Lily wakes up and wonders where you are?"

"She probably won't," Bella said. "But I left her a note."

He still wasn't able to figure out a good reason why she'd abandoned her quest for reading material and was braving the storm with him instead. The last woman he'd dated—Gwen—definitely had ulterior motives, and it was hard to trust that wasn't the case with every woman.

But he wasn't dating Bella. Not even close.

They reached the shed, and to his relief, none of the horses appeared unusually troubled by the storm. He walked from stall to stall, making soothing noises.

"You're good with them," Bella observed. "What were you going to tell Lily about your experiences with horses?"

She was Lily's mother, of course she would ask.

"It was one horse," Luke replied, "and one experience."

Briefly he recounted his encounter with the horse who had gone wild. Even telling it caused his heart to race with remembering. His whole body shuddered at how badly it could have ended.

"Maybe Lily doesn't need to hear that," he said.

"She won't forget that you said you would tell her," Bella said. "Besides, I think she'll admire you."

"For what?"

"For doing something you need to do, even though you're afraid. That's actually a great lesson for her—for anyone."

Luke wanted to protest that he wasn't afraid. What kind of image was that for a ranch owner to have?

But something in Bella's expression said that she respected him too.

What are her fears, Lord?

It hadn't escaped him how rapidly and firmly she'd slammed the door on any questions about Lily's father. Maybe they'd had a bad marriage. Well, obviously something wasn't right, or he'd still be in the picture.

But there was no point speculating on that. He had a ranch to save, and the only role that Bella played in his life was that, according to her claims, she would be the one to help him do so.

"If you still think it's okay, I'll fill Lily in like I told her I would," Luke said.

"Of course," Bella said. "Lily isn't…" She hesitated, tugging absent-mindedly at a strand of rain-soaked hair. "I mean, she doesn't need to be protected from things." She chuckled ruefully. "I guess I'm reminding myself of that as much as anyone. She's had kind of a rough go lately. She's an extreme introvert. You maybe don't see it because she likes you—and that's kind of a big deal, by the way—and she's committed to learning more about the horses. But with people and situations she's uncomfortable with…it's not good."

"I will do everything in my power to make sure that this experience lives up to her expectations," Luke said.

"I know you're doing your best," Bella said. "But, if I'm being honest, you need more to draw people in, something that makes it stand out, like if they were just driving by on the highway, what would make them want to turn their cars in? Maybe a bigger sign? Something flashier…"

"I thought your concern was with your daughter," Luke couldn't resist saying, just so Bella would stop going on about gaudy signs set up on his family property.

She studied his face for a moment. Then, as if she'd decided it was best to change the subject, said, "They seem to be okay," indicating the horses. "I probably should get back up."

"Do you still need something to read? If you tell me what

you like, I could bring out a selection," Luke suggested, a bit uneasy at the way he'd reacted and trying to amend things.

She shook her head, almost like her original reason for coming up to the house had been forgotten.

"Thank you, but I think I can sleep now."

"Okay, great," Luke said. But an unexpected twinge of disappointment lingered, which was silly because he wasn't going to suggest they continue to hang out in the stables getting to know each other better.

Was he?

"See, I told you, Lily." Alison's slow, mocking voice from the doorway made both Luke and Bella jump. "I told you they'd sneaked off somewhere together."

Chapter Eight

Even though Luke had quickly squashed the "sneaking off" comment the night before, Bella's stomach still knotted slightly as she waited for Lily to wake up.

As they'd walked back up to their cabin together, with Luke and Alison following behind, Lily's silence had a judgmental stoniness to it, and she remained silent, going back to her bed and pulling the covers over her head.

Or was she just imagining the judgment, Bella wondered, because she felt guilty? She really had started out with the simple intention of finding something to read. But ending up in the stable with Luke during the storm, now that she saw it from her daughter's perspective, did seem to have a slightly clandestine quality to it.

She was anxious for Lily to wake up so she could assure her that she had no interest in Luke other than as her daughter's therapy horse trainer.

Aside from that, she really did have an urge to make this ranch everything her expertise told her it could be, an urge that was, somehow, only strengthened by Luke's push back against it. Even though he'd said he would listen to her ideas, it was clear he didn't want to.

She wasn't exactly sure what that meant. Perhaps she just needed the satisfaction of seeing her ideas come to fruition…or to prove to herself that she was still marketable if she couldn't continue working where she was.

Bella's meandering thoughts came to a halt like a runaway freight train colliding into a mountain.

No, Lily had absolutely nothing to worry about when it came to her and Luke. There was no way she was looking for a relationship with him or anyone else. Everyone could put up a good front until the chips were down, even handsome, stormy-eyed ranchers who had their own fears. Even if they shared their umbrella, offered to deliver books to you and had your shy daughter's stamp of approval.

As it turned out, her fretting as she waited for Lily to wake up was all for nothing. The only concern on her daughter's mind was if the aftermath of the storm would impact her lesson that day.

"They need an indoor arena for contingencies like this," Bella said and made a mental note. Reminding herself that she had taken on the role of advisor helped focus her thoughts so that they wouldn't stray into dangerous territory.

Where the money would come from for an extra like an indoor arena, she had no idea. She was puzzled that the ranch was in the state it was in. All the trophies, photos and newspaper and magazine accolades that were liberally displayed in the areas throughout the house she'd seen would point to the place being successful.

What had gone wrong?

But she wasn't a financial advisor and didn't pretend to be. Her role was to help clients see potential and find ways to maximize it.

She never got emotionally involved and wasn't about to start now.

The thunder and lightning had abated, but the rain continued in a light but persistent fashion. So when they all gathered at the breakfast table, it was clear that a backup plan was needed for the day.

"Can we go into Trydale?" Alison asked. "Get lunch at the café? Look at the shops?"

"That's actually not a bad idea," Luke said. "How would you all feel about a trip into town?"

"I can't go," Nora said immediately. Her eyes clouded over as she took an anxious sip of her orange juice.

"Can't go, Mom?" Luke prodded gently. "Or don't want to?"

Nora pasted on what Bella could tell was a practiced smile. It was the smile of a woman who was used to putting up a good front.

"I don't think it's necessary to suggest anything remiss in front of our guests, Lucas," she said. "I have some things I need to do."

Bella could tell Luke wanted to ask more questions. His eyes narrowed in a way that said he didn't quite believe her claim. But apparently, he also knew better than to push because he said, "I guess it will be the four of us then. That is—" he glanced in Bella's direction "—if you and Lily are up for it?"

Lily was already nodding her head.

With a plan in the works, the mood around the table lightened. Alison chatted in a friendly way to Lily about colors and styles she thought would look good on her.

Bella wasn't sure how she felt about Alison styling her daughter, but it was good to see them getting along. At least it was one less thing to worry about for the summer.

"You don't have pierced ears, do you?" Alison asked, leaning sideways in her chair to inspect Lily's earlobes. "Won't your mom let you?"

"She said it was my choice," Lily answered. "I don't really see the point."

"The point is that you get to buy a bunch of cool earrings that go with your clothes."

The girls argued but in a good-natured way.

Bella smiled. Lily did love a good argument, a side that not many got to see.

Nora gave a small sniff, a noise that could have meant any number of things, none of which Bella cared to find out. The older woman excused herself and took her tea into another room.

"Can I be excused too?" Alison asked. "I need to get ready." She looked at Bella. "Can Lily come to my room?"

"Sure," Bella said. "But remember you need to get ready too, Lil."

Lily nodded and the girls bounded off.

With the girls and Nora gone, the kitchen seemed suddenly too quiet to Bella.

Luke jiggled his coffee cup around a little, pensively studying the remaining contents. He cleared his throat.

"Are you okay with the girls shopping together?" he asked into the silence. "Were you planning to go with Lily? If you're okay with them browsing a bit on their own, I'd love to buy you coffee at the True to You café. They serve the best cup of coffee you've ever had. I know everyone says that, but I challenge you to tell me any differently once you've tried it. If our timing's right, Jacob might have some bannock on hand. For sure he'll have Saskatoon berry muffins. We could also talk more about your ideas for the ranch."

"I'm sure it will be fine," Bella said. "We drove through Trydale on the way here, and it looks like a lovely small town, everything close by. I'm sure the shops wouldn't be too far from that coffee shop, right?" She wondered if she was trying to convince Luke or herself.

"I don't know much about earrings," Luke said in a droll

way that made Bella smile. "But there's a clothing store right across the street and a bookstore next door, so you can stock up if you want to."

"You know me well," Bella said with a smile.

What am I doing?

It almost seemed like she was flirting with Luke, but she didn't flirt, ever. She never did anything that could be remotely construed as flirting, not since that night.

"We don't have to go for coffee if you think it's a bad idea," Luke said anxiously. "I'm not trying to talk you out of shopping."

The sickening memory of that night had curdled Bella's stomach, and the distaste must have shown on her face. She didn't want Luke to think there was something wrong with her or lose the opportunity to make an impression at the ranch.

If word got out that she was able to turn things around for a place that seemed dangerously close to going out of business, chances were good—or at least better—that she would be able to say no to Felicity and her unscrupulous client and still be able to make a living.

"Coffee sounds fine," she said in her business voice. "I'd better go get ready."

"Meet you at my car in fifteen?" Luke said. "Is that long enough?"

"Yes."

She didn't plan to fuss with her appearance.

"Come on, Lily," she called out, perhaps louder than was necessary, but her nerves were jangled.

A few seconds later, Lily and Alison appeared. Alison looked amused, but her daughter's delicate features were marred by an annoyed frown.

"We have to get ready to go," Bella said, willing herself to a calmer tone. "Luke wants to leave in fifteen minutes."

Almost on schedule, they were in Luke's dark gray SUV and headed toward Trydale.

The girls scrambled into the back seat and Alison immediately began scrolling her phone for music. She plugged in headphones and handed one earbud to Lily.

Bella thought about asking what they were listening to but decided better of it. Lily had not enjoyed many bonding experiences with kids her own age over the past while, and maybe this was a fresh start.

She just wished Alison's attitude was a little better. But maybe Lily, who had a strong sense of who she was, despite her shyness, would be good for her.

She wondered if Luke's brother was anything like him. She slid a look at Luke out of the corner of her eye.

His eyes were on the road, his sun-browned and roughened hands steady on the steering wheel, with a firm grip. He drove like he loved to drive, Bella mused, but also like he respected the task.

Luke must have felt her gaze because he swiveled his head for a quick glance in her direction.

"Everything okay?"

"Yes," Bella said. "You're a good driver." Part of her wished she could swallow back the latter statement. She rarely offered a compliment to a man, unless it involved a project they were working on together.

"Thank you," Luke said, his eyes back on the road.

On the way to the ranch, Bella had been too focused on the driving and watching for signs to pay much attention to the surrounding area.

The land around Trydale was fertile, encouraging a variety of abundant crops. The Saskatchewan summer showed off its stunning greenery and a blue sky that had as many personalities as the land itself.

Luke slowed the car to town speed as they approached the sign that said Welcome to Trydale! You're Part of the Family Here.

As always, the change in speed made it seem for a moment like they were going turtle slow.

Alison and Lily pulled out their earbuds, and Alison said to Lily, "Let's go shopping."

"Not quite yet," Luke said, saving Bella the trouble.

"We'll pop in at Jacob's place first," he continued, "and come up with our game plan."

"Game plan," Alison repeated, wrinkling her nose. But a pointed look from her uncle stopped her from saying more.

"It'll be good," Lily spoke up. "I'm kind of thirsty anyway."

Luke wheeled the car into a parking spot on Main Street and pointed. "Café is right up here," he said.

Bella looked in the direction he was pointing and liked what she saw. The café combined small-town vibes with an aesthetic that showed a strong sense of Indigenous culture. A brightly colored mural showing respect and love for nature adorned the side of the building.

Bella thought that it echoed Luke's love for the land and nature that surrounded the ranch.

It would be good if, on neutral ground, they could make some decisions together that would benefit both of them.

Maybe it would be good if they could come to a deeper understanding of each other in general.

The instant he opened the door to the True to You café, a sense of warmth and welcome settled on Luke, calming the jitterbugs that danced in his stomach while he drove with a beautiful woman beside him.

What was it about Bella that made him so aware or, to be more specific, so aware that she was aware of him?

He didn't think for one second that she was interested in him. She was watchful, almost scrutinizing, like she was trying to figure him out. It could have to do with the fact that he was largely responsible for her daughter's experiences that summer, but he didn't think it was just that.

Now he found himself seeing Jacob Amyott's café through her eyes. A loyalty to the place that had nourished him physically and emotionally swelled up in him.

If she doesn't love everything about this place, then she's not someone I would trust with the future of my family home.

"Be right out," Jacob's deep voice called from the back.

"Take your time, Jacob," Luke called back.

"Luke Duffy." A six-foot-four Indigenous man came out from behind a deep orange curtain, clutching three stacked wooden crates filled with jars of jam against his chest and wearing a smile that beamed an openhearted welcome.

Jacob was nearing his eighties but still had impeccable posture and radiated strength and energy. He wore blue jeans and a black shirt with a royal blue beaded pattern on it. His white hair was short at the front, but when he turned around, it hung halfway down his back in a braid.

"You've brought company," Jacob remarked, as his kind, shrewd eyes swept over them.

It suddenly occurred to Luke that Jacob and Bella had that kind of watchfulness in common. But he sensed that Bella's watchfulness was to prepare herself to shut people out, whereas Jacob was always seeking a way to usher them in.

"Yes, this is my niece, Alison." Luke laid a hand on her shoulder.

"Brett's girl." Jacob nodded. "Nice to see you again."

Alison smiled politely. "You too."

"And this is Bella Lark and her daughter, Lily. They are guests at the ranch this summer."

"Ahh, a good place to be." Jacob nodded. "What do you like best about it?"

He directed his question to Lily in that non-pressuring Jacob way that made it easy for even the shy Lily to respond to him.

"Definitely the horses."

"Good choice. They are magnificent creatures. Please sit anywhere you like," Jacob said. "You came at the right time."

Luke knew that soon the popular café would begin to fill up with regulars and, since it was summer, also with tourists that had heard of its reputation for delicious food and a friendly proprietor.

They ordered a stack of the Saskatoon berry pancakes to share, along with sides of Canadian bacon and breakfast sausage and plenty of maple syrup to accompany it all.

Jacob brought out mugs of the much-lauded coffee for Luke and Bella, while the girls chose apple juice and exclaimed over its tart, fresh taste and went into rhapsodies over the pancakes.

Luke noted with amusement that good food and drink had edged out the urge for an immediate shopping trip.

Luke watched Bella take her first sip of the coffee and found pleasure in watching her mild skepticism disappear as she first widened her eyes as all the nuances of the flavor hit her taste buds and then closed them to savor the moment.

"Okay," Bella said, opening her eyes and taking another sip. "You were right. That is absolutely the best coffee I've ever had. I don't suppose you'd give up your secret?" she asked Jacob.

"You would be correct on that," Jacob said, but he smiled at her, and without hesitation, she smiled back, an open smile.

Luke noticed that Bella had different kinds of smiles. There was the tight-lipped, polite one that he could easily picture her using with her clients. There was the loving, slightly anxious one that Lily brought out in her. There was a slightly smug one when she had proven herself right about something…and there was this one.

The warm and natural one that he rarely saw and couldn't help wishing could be bestowed on him more often.

She's a guest. She's just a guest.

As soon as the girls swallowed their last bites, washed down with the delicious apple juice, Alison began to clamor to go shopping again.

"If you're sure that's what you want to do?" Bella asked Lily.

Her anxious smile was back.

"Sure, it'll be fun," Lily said.

They agreed that they could go across the street to the shops for no more than an hour. Luke and Bella would remain at the café and talk about the ranch.

"I could manage another cup of that coffee too," Bella said after the girls had departed, chatting excitedly about their ex-pedition.

Jacob refilled their mugs again and then went to get menus and greet another group of hungry customers who had just come in.

"So," Luke said, "what do you think of this place? It's something, isn't it?"

Viewing the True to You café as objectively as he could manage, he was aware that, in many ways, it wasn't all that different from most small-town cafés: there were stools lining the counter, booths at tables with marks and scratches in the wood that told silent stories, paintings on the wall that could feature in any small-town restaurant, a jukebox that could still rasp out some heart-wrenching tunes…

The biggest draw was Jacob, the love he poured into the

food he prepared and the kindness and respect he showed to the people he served it to.

Being kind and doing his best work day by day was a tribute he paid to his beloved Bertha, who had passed away after a brief, no-holds-barred fight with cancer many years ago.

Jacob kept her memory and her passion for food and people alive as diligently as he could.

"It's a great place for sure," Bella said. She picked up a menu again and scanned it. Her eyes narrowed, scrutinizing, and a smile of dawning realization broke across her face.

"What is it?" Luke asked.

"There are quotes about food from literary classics embedded in the menu," Bella said. "I can't believe I didn't notice that before."

"Oh, that's right," Luke said. "I know that. I guess I never think about it anymore because I'm here so much. Jacob has a degree in classic literature," he added.

"Wow, that's impressive," Bella said.

"Some people, when they find that out, wonder why he's just running a diner."

"There's nothing 'just' about this," Bella retorted with a ferocity that surprised but pleased Luke.

"I agree," he said eagerly. "There are things that Jacob and this place give to people that you can't teach out of books. But if anyone wants to chat great literature with him, he's more than willing. He'll be happy that you noticed the menus."

Bella nodded and resumed studying hers.

Luke found himself wishing that they could continue on with this type of conversation and he could forget his worries about what was happening at New Hope.

Just chat like we are really friends…

"This is actually a good way to make the points I want to make about your ranch," Bella said, quickly shattering Luke's brief thought that they could pretend they were there on a friendly outing.

"When you look around here," Bella continued, taking on what Luke had come to think of as her business voice, "you can see that Jacob is very clear on what his brand is. He loves literature, he loves his culture, and he shows both of those things in an unmistakable way. Now, what would you say the ranch's brand is?"

Luke blinked at her. What was all this brand talk? He highly doubted that Jacob ever thought of what he did here in the café as a brand.

"Well..." he began slowly. "It's, uh, my home. It's where I grew up."

The door to the café opened and let in a summer breeze that briefly stirred up the baked goods, savory meats and woodsy pine smell that would forever bring this café to Luke's memory.

Luke glanced in the direction of the door, grateful for the reprieve, and saw a woman who wasn't familiar to him.

She looked younger than him and Bella, as far as he could tell. She was of medium height and had a slight but still strong-looking frame. She wore blue jeans and a plaid shirt, had golden-brown eyes and dark hair that framed her slightly pointed chin.

"Aubrey." Jacob spotted her and waved her over to the table. "Luke," he said, "this is Aubrey Simpson. She's been living here in Trydale for a few months now. By all accounts, she's a fine horse trainer. I wanted her to meet you. You know, just in case you have need for one at your ranch."

Luke stood up and shook her hand. "This is Bella," he said. "She's a guest at the ranch right now."

He had to trust his face to maintain a polite smile while his thoughts reminded him that Jacob didn't know about the financial troubles they were having at the ranch, thus wouldn't know how unlikely it was that he'd be hiring anyone new.

Jacob stood by beaming while they all introduced themselves, and Luke wondered if having guests at New Hope reinforced the false idea that they were doing better than they actually were.

He'd never discussed any of it with Jacob because he still needed a place he could go to that gave him a break from those worries.

"Nice to meet you both," Aubrey said. "I just popped in for a few minutes to pick up one of Jacob's superb takeout lunches in a bag." She looked questioningly at Luke. "I could leave you my business card?"

Luke nodded, asking himself what else he could do. He took the card and pretended to study it.

Jacob went and got a brown bag and handed it to Aubrey along with a bottle of chocolate milk.

"Hope to hear from you," Aubrey said brightly as she headed out the door.

Again, Luke nodded.

When he placed the card carefully facedown on the table, he looked up to find Bella contemplating him.

Okay, Lord, I get it. We're not here as friends or to just have a fun conversation. The ranch needs saving.

Luke gave Bella a shrug. "I wasn't sure what else to do," he said.

"No, I totally get that," she said. She paused, thoughtfully tapping her nails on the side of the coffee mug. "Would you hire another horse trainer if you could?"

"In a heartbeat." Luke didn't add that he would also gladly get rid of Cal Wayman if it meant the wage they paid him— far too high by Luke's way of thinking—could be funneled into things and people who would actually benefit the ranch.

He didn't even want to say Cal's name, as if doing so would bring a dark cloud on this pleasant outing.

"Let's make that your horizon goal then." Bella took a flowered notebook and matching pen out of her purse.

"My what?"

"Your horizon goal," Bella repeated, her blue eyes lighting up with pleasure over starting a plan.

She has such lovely eyes...

She continued explaining, and Luke made himself pay attention.

"That's what I call the goal that's currently out of reach, or at least seems out of reach, but you can still see it—you know it's out there. So your horizon goal would be to make New Hope successful enough that you can consider hiring a new horse trainer."

She wrote something down with a flourish.

For a moment, Luke caught Bella's wave of optimism and determination, but then reality hit.

"I hate to muddy the waters," he said, "but that seems to me more like a vicious circle goal."

"Why do you say that?"

"Because we need more trainers to bring enough people in, and we can't afford more trainers *until* more people come in."

"We can figure this out, Luke," Bella said.

The "we" almost made him feel like they were partners, until she added, "That's what I do. It's how I make my living."

No, they weren't partners, and they weren't really friends.

They were simply two people who had their own agendas.

Even if he was starting to wish it could be more.

Chapter Nine

It didn't seem to matter how persistently Bella's inner voice tried to remind her that she didn't, and couldn't, trust men, a stronger urge surged through.

She wanted to do whatever she could to bring that look of optimism and hope back to Luke's face. She wanted him to believe—to *know*—that New Hope could be saved.

She wanted to believe it herself, and she wanted to be part of it.

There was something about seeing Luke in what he had described as one of his favorite places, interacting with a man he cared for and looked up to. She felt, somehow, like she could see the boy he had been inside the rugged, sun-browned-skin exterior.

It made her wonder what his relationship with his own father had been. She realized that, although he had mentioned his father, there was always a shadow alongside of it, and she wondered why.

She'd certainly witnessed the strain between him and Nora, and his brother appeared to have abandoned Luke to juggle the chips that were falling.

"You're quiet," Luke remarked. "I guess I've put a damper on your ideas, but I'm just being realistic."

"I'm just thinking," Bella said. "There's got to be a solution. There always is."

She decided that when she had more time to focus, she would run through her client list to see if she could come up with anyone who might have ideas or connections that could help.

She would never in a million years say so, but she was also thinking about how she could have missed those notes of gravel and honey in his voice. Luke could at times have a boyish vulnerability to him, but he was definitely all man with that lean but muscular build, the scruff of whiskers on his chin and the brooding look in his eyes that somehow made his grin, when it appeared, even more defined and heart-catching.

What am I doing?

To distract herself, Bella looked around the restaurant. The tables were full now; it had happened without her noticing.

"I'm also thinking we should order something else," she said in a crisp way. "We're taking up a table, and it's getting busy in here."

"Jacob doesn't mind," Luke said. "He likes people to know they're welcome to stay as long as they like. Besides—" he checked the time on his phone "—the girls should be back any minute."

Lily.

Bella realized that for the last little while she hadn't even thought about her daughter. While it was good for her to acknowledge that Lily was growing up and needed more independence, Bella wasn't happy with herself that she had allowed Luke to be such a distraction.

"Here they come now," Luke said, looking out the window.

As soon as Lily and Alison entered the café, Bella knew her daughter wasn't happy.

She wondered for a moment if Alison had tried to push her into something she wasn't comfortable with, but the girls sat across from each other and happily discussed the purchases

they'd made, which seemed mainly to consist of various fla-
vored lip glosses and bracelets woven out of bright thread.
They'd also each got sequined purses that changed their shim-
mering hues when they brushed the sequins the other way.

Bella felt hypnotized for a moment, watching the colors
change from silver to blue and back again.

"Looks like the skies are clearing," Luke said. "Who's
ready to get back to the ranch?"

"Me!" Lily said, waving her hand, causing Bella to wonder if she'd imagined her daughter's demeanor when she'd
first come in.

"No book?" she asked Lily as the girls gathered their new
purchases.

"I don't have to get a book every single time," Lily snapped.

Okay, so she is upset about something.

"No, you don't have to," Bella said, lowering her voice,
"but you usually love to."

She let Luke and Alison get a few steps ahead of them.
"What's wrong?" she whispered.

"I don't want to talk about it."

"Is it Alison?" Bella mouthed and discreetly pointed.

"No," Lily said, infusing her whisper with as much annoy-
ance as possible. "I'm mad at you."

"Me? What for?"

Luke looked over his shoulder then to see if they were following, and Bella quickly adjusted her face into what she
hoped was a neutral expression, thankful that she'd had years
of experience in tough client meetings.

But Luke's raised eyebrow showed he wasn't buying it,
though all he said was "Coming, ladies?"

Lily flipped her ponytail over her shoulder, and Bella
watched it sway as she stalked ahead of her mother, putting
distance between them.

She wondered what it would be like to have a partner with whom to discuss a moody preteen. That she would go there, even in her thoughts, was almost as puzzling to her as Lily's anger.

She didn't have a chance to quiz Lily further on the drive home, as she and Alison plugged in the earbuds again.

"Everything okay with you and your daughter?" Luke asked in a quiet voice as he drove. "You can tell me it's none of my business, but I just thought I sensed some tension between you back at the café."

Bella exhaled thoughtfully. Maybe it wasn't any of Luke's business, but still, it was thoughtful of him to notice.

Maybe there were men who could think about more than what they wanted and taking it at any cost. Of course, there had to be. Every day she saw doting husbands and fathers; her own father was a decent man. She just had to keep her mind closed to the possibility and keep herself emotionally distant because it was the only thing that kept the memory of that night from destroying her.

"I'm sorry. I've crossed a line," Luke said, misconstruing her silence.

"No, not at all," Bella hurried to reassure him. "I appreciate you asking, but I don't think I should get into it now." She darted her eyes up to the rearview mirror.

Lily's eyes met hers in the mirror, and a scowl appeared to wrinkle her forehead.

"To be honest," Bella said to Luke, dropping her eyes, "I have no idea what's going on, but apparently she's upset with me about something."

Luke nodded then, after a few seconds, he continued their low-voiced conversation. "I think Lily has been good for Alison."

"Really?" Bella was pleased Luke would think so.

"Yeah, did you notice that she looks different today? More like someone her age should look?"

"I did notice," Bella said. "She's a beautiful girl."

"Lily too."

Luke turned his head briefly, offering the gentle smile of a shared moment. Her heart pulsed in an unfamiliar way.

"It's like it's taking forever to get back," Lily suddenly complained from the back seat.

As Bella had suspected, her daughter was paying attention and was making it clear that she didn't like what she saw.

Is she mad at me because she thinks there's something between Luke and me?

Bella's thoughts raced. Was it possible that Lily actually believed she was striking up some kind of relationship and was worried it would change everything? Well, if Lily was worried about that, Bella could quickly put her mind at ease.

For the remainder of the drive, she looked out the window, carefully avoiding any urge to look in Luke's direction, and chatted about some of her most successful PR campaigns.

Luke remained silent, nodding occasionally as she talked. When Bella finally looked at him as they all got out of the car, she could see he was puzzled.

She reminded herself that she didn't owe him an explanation about her changeable behavior. They were guests, and he was their host.

Her goals were that Lily have a great summer that would give her the needed boost to face school in the fall, and to get Luke to the point where he was at least willing to see what the ranch's potential was.

But she thought about the baffled, slightly sorrowful, look on his face when she'd tried to talk to him about brand and something like an invisible elbow nudged her insides, telling her he was not her typical client. But she would figure it out.

She had to.

Out of the car, Lily turned and started making a beeline for their cabin, not even waiting to see if Alison wanted to continue hanging out. But Alison seemed to take it all in stride, so Bella guessed they must have talked about it in the car on the drive home.

"Aren't you going to thank Luke for taking us into town?" Bella called after her.

"Thank you," Lily said over her shoulder and kept going.

"I need to go have a little chat with my daughter," Bella said.

Luke nodded. "Just come up to the house whenever she wants to see Hooligan again. Come on, Alison." He put an arm lightly around his niece's shoulder, and Bella thought she might shrug it off, but instead the corners of her mouth lifted in a small smile at the show of affection.

It made her heart tug with a dangerous ache. She couldn't allow herself to think that Lily was missing something in her life by not having a father figure. The two of them had always done just fine on their own.

Anxious to find out what had provoked Lily's animosity toward her, Bella had turned to go back to their cabin but stopped only a short distance away from the house when she heard Luke's voice again, this time tight with his own animosity toward someone.

"Mom, what's he doing here?"

Curious, Bella paused and turned back to see Nora, her usually distant expression lit up with a kind of defiance, standing on the front porch of the house with Cal Wayman coming up behind her.

"I work here, remember?" Cal said in a dry way, but with too much of an edge to be truly humorous.

Again Bella felt the chill of instinctive dislike she experienced around him. It was more than her usual caution around most men—she was sure that Cal Wayman was *not* a good person.

"You don't work inside the house," Luke pointed out, his shoulders lifting and falling with agitated breaths.

Bella had a sudden urge to go and stand with him, to offer her silent support.

But no, this was none of her business, and she never had and never would put her concern for someone else ahead of her concern for Lily.

"I invited Cal here," she heard Nora say, as she turned and continued on. "He was Sly's right-hand man, and if I want his opinion on something, it's my right to ask for it."

Bella couldn't hear any more, but her curiosity burned. She could only imagine what Luke would reply, but she was with him on this one: she didn't trust Cal Wayman at all and worried that the emotionally fragile Nora apparently did.

Bella forced any thoughts of the Duffys' issues out of her mind as she opened the cabin door.

Lily lay on her bed—she had chosen the one nearest the window—and stared at the ceiling as she repeatedly tossed a small cushion up, catching it as it fell.

"What happened in town?" Bella asked, getting right to the point.

Lily sighed and folded her arms across her chest, letting the cushion fall beside her on the bed.

"I don't want to tell you," she said.

"Is it something about Alison?" Bella persisted. "Is it something she did or said? You can tell me."

"It's not Alison!" Lily yelled in frustration. "It's you."

She sat up quickly and drew up her knees, wrapping her arms around them and burying her head.

"If you read people as well as you always say you do," she

continued, her voice muffled so that Bella had to strain to hear, "you'd know that Alison isn't a bad person. She's hurt that her parents left her here and don't even seem to miss her. So I don't know why you have to assume what's going in is her fault."

I'm sorry, Lord, Bella said in a silent prayer. *I know that seeing the bad in people is not how You would have us behave.*

"So, she's talked about her parents with you?" Bella asked softly.

Lily lifted her head. "We've already talked about a lot of things."

Bella nodded. Sometime soon, she would ask about those conversations, and she vowed she would be a good, positive listener. But right now, she still didn't have an answer for her original question.

"You still haven't told me why you're mad at me," she said.

Lily stood up and paced the room back and forth, tugging at the end of her hair with one hand, a sure sign of agitation.

"Lil?"

Lily stopped and glared at her. "Why won't you tell me anything about my dad? Alison was telling me all about her parents, and she asked me about my dad, and I couldn't tell her *anything*. Not where he is, not whether he's alive or dead, not even his name. Do you realize how weird that is?" she demanded.

Bella swallowed a sickish bile that her suddenly churning stomach sent up to her throat. She hadn't fully realized how much she yearned for this subject not to scar their time here until now.

Yes, Lily had been more frequently showing curiosity and asking more questions but so far had been willing to let Bella distract her with vague answers or a complete change in topic.

"We're a great team," Bella would often say. "We're doing great, just the two of us."

But now, as Lily paced and the words that poured out of her mouth increased in speed, hurt and anger, Bella realized she would have to come up with a better answer.

But I can't possibly tell her the truth. Father God, what am I supposed to do?

The knock at the door startled Bella, and she saw Lily physically close herself off by folding her arms across her chest and looking down at her feet.

Bella briefly considered ignoring the knock, but then Luke's voice said, "Bella? Lily? I was wondering if you were ready to spend some time with the horses?"

Without looking at her, Lily dashed across the room and opened the door.

"Let's go," she said rather unceremoniously, not waiting for her mother's consent.

Luke's gaze met hers over Lily's head.

"Everything okay?" he mouthed.

Bella gave her head a brief shake, but out loud she said, "Sure, it will be nice to get outside. Let's go."

Lily mumbled that she didn't want Bella to join them, which Bella chose to ignore.

She knew she should have reined in her reaction and not acknowledged to Luke, even slightly, that there was anything wrong. But, in that moment, she was mostly just grateful for the reprieve.

She knew it wouldn't last long though. Lily wasn't a little girl anymore, and she wouldn't forget that she wanted answers.

From the moment Lily flung open the cabin door, Luke knew that he'd intruded into a situation fraught with tension. He got a strong impression that it was something more than a typical mother-daughter quarrel—or whatever he imagined one of those would be. He was no expert. But he sensed that he stumbled upon something that carried a history of pain with it.

He also noticed as they walked to the stables that Bella paced her steps so that she wasn't walking either with him or Lily. She appeared to be lost in her own thoughts. The after-storm breeze lifted and played gently with her pretty hair, and he let himself enjoy the sight.

His mother had refused to tell him why she'd invited Cal up to the house, but she hadn't thought to put away the folders on the dining room table and grew defensive when Luke asked about them.

"Mom," he had said, "please tell me that you're not discussing any of our financial affairs, or anything at all, with Cal Wayman."

"If I was, it would be my business," his mother had retorted.

Frustration and anger bloomed in Luke, unfurling like a poisonous flower. He was filled with the immediate need to distance himself from the situation before he said words that could never be taken back, which was how he'd found himself at the door of their guests' cabin.

He only now thought that he should have asked Alison to come along.

Luke assumed that Bella wouldn't want him asking any questions, so he was surprised when she asked one of her own.

"Was everything okay up at the house?"

He darted a look in her direction, but she kept her eyes straight ahead, fixed on Lily's back as the girl sprinted ahead of them.

"What makes you ask?"

There was no doubt he was more attracted to Bella than he wanted to be, and he experienced moments when he believed she understood him and his situation, but, ultimately, she was a guest at New Hope, and even if she and Lily weren't, he never considered it appropriate to publicly vent about his family's issues.

Maybe he had more of Sly Duffy's family pride in him than he thought.

He looked at Bella, still waiting for her answer.

"I saw that Cal was up at the house," she told him. "I get the feeling that you don't trust him."

Luke drew in a breath but then simply nodded. He couldn't even pretend to deny that.

"I don't either," Bella said simply.

Immediately, a protective instinct surged through him so rapidly and intensely it stopped him in his tracks and he spun to face Bella, touching her arm briefly to stop her progress too.

"Has he said something to you?" he demanded. "Done something?"

He could see that Bella was taken aback by his intensity— *Great, now I'm scaring her*—and he made himself soften his tone and relax his body posture.

"I just mean that you are a guest here, and if Cal—if anyone— is doing anything to spoil your time here, you have to let me know so I can do something about it."

Bella met his gaze, and he thought that her eyes told more stories than she would ever speak, and not just about Cal.

He wondered again what he had come across when he'd gone to their cabin.

"He hasn't done or said anything," she finally answered. "I just know the type." A note of acute pain dashed into her eyes.

Then Luke could see her shedding her vulnerability, like it was an unwanted cloak that didn't protect her against the elements, and she was all business again.

"We still need to really talk about our game plan here."

"Are you coming, Luke?" Lily's plaintive voice coming from inside the stable shook him out of his speculations.

The truth was, he really didn't know what was going on with Bella, and there was no point imagining himself being a prince riding to the rescue on a white horse when, number one, she hadn't asked him to, and, number two, he had enough to rescue when it came to the ranch and his mother, and the white horse was already lame.

"Yes, be right there," Luke answered.

Bella hesitated in the entrance.

"Coming?" he invited.

She didn't quite pull off a laugh. "I'm not sure she wants me."

Lily stood stroking Hooligan's nose, remaining gentle with him while her eyes snapped impatience. Still, the large animal, being the intuitive creature he was, snorted and stepped back and forth a bit.

"Can I try riding him today?" Lily asked.

Luke didn't mean to, but he instinctively sought Bella's reaction.

Lily saw it too and frowned. "You told me that it was always up to the trainer and the pupil to decide what they're ready to try," she reminded him.

"I did say that," Luke hedged. "But you're a minor, so I can't go against your mother's wishes either."

It was interesting, he thought, the way he could already tell when Bella was weighing out a decision, trying to draw the best solution out of difficult options.

"Do you think you're ready for that, Lil?"

Lily nodded vigorously. Whatever their earlier issues had been, it appeared that Lily wasn't going to push any boundaries when it came to getting permission to go riding.

Still, Luke wanted to make doubly sure for all of their sakes.

"You don't have to be in any rush, Lil," Luke said, noticing that he'd picked up her mother's way of addressing her.

He hoped they wouldn't mind. "You've really only been with Hoolie a few times, and there's still plenty we can do before you start riding him. You've got the rest of the summer, and some people never ride the horses at all."

"I want to ride him," Lily said firmly. "I know I'm ready. Plus, me and Alison want to go riding together."

"Just as long as Alison isn't pressuring you into this," Luke said, with a certainty that he was echoing Bella's thoughts.

Lily gave a massive eye roll that reminded him of his niece.

"You sound like my mom," she complained. "I don't know why everyone thinks that Alison is going to be this bad influence on me. Maybe you should pay more attention to what's really going on with her, and you'd realize she just needs friends."

Luke carried a vague guilt around with him over failing to please his father while he was alive, not knowing how to save New Hope from going under, and his frustration with his mother. Guilt was a perpetual, sometimes almost unnoticed companion, but at Lily's words it sharpened, jabbing him from all sides and making itself impossible to ignore.

"She's just having a bad day," Bella's voice said beside him, low so that only he could hear. "It's me she's upset with, not you."

It gave Luke a sense of being bonded to someone, feeling support that he hadn't felt in a long time.

It took him a moment to notice that Bella had laid her hand on his arm, a touch to punctuate her words and to reassure him. They seemed to notice it at the same time, and he was just beginning to savor the connection when she yanked her hand back like something had burned it.

When he looked at her, though, he couldn't quite read her expression. It seemed more puzzled than anything, as if she didn't understand her own actions.

"Luke, can you please help me?" Lily huffed out impatiently. It was time to get down to business.

He demonstrated how to put a saddle on Hooligan then watched her do it herself a few times until she had it down pat. Thankfully, Hoolie was a relatively easy horse to saddle, not prone to tensing his abdominal muscles as some did when they wanted to control the tightening of the cinch.

He encouraged Lily to lead the horse out of the barn to the training field. He prayed as they walked that he wasn't making a mistake letting her get on the horse. But surely her mother would have stepped in and said something if she'd seen a problem with it. Bella wasn't shy about saying when she didn't like something.

Something nagged at him, however, that said that Bella wasn't entirely herself since they'd gotten back from their visit in town. Other than asking Lily if she really believed she was ready to ride, she'd remained uncharacteristically silent on the matter, appearing instead to be troubled by whatever tension was between her and Lily when he'd knocked on their door.

"I promise I'll keep a close eye on things," Luke told her as they followed Lily and Hooligan.

"I know you will."

The simple declaration of trust warmed him.

Outside, the air was cleansed and seemed brand new after the storm. The prairie sky above them was vast and blue, accented by soft gray clouds whispering into the wind, no longer holding any threat.

Luke took a pause to close his eyes, breathe and be thankful for the creation around him.

When he opened his eyes again, Bella was gazing at him with a small smile, one he hadn't seen from her before.

It was the smile of a kindred spirit.

She too took in the surroundings and made an open-armed gesture, like she wanted to embrace them.

"Kind of makes you wonder how people can doubt there's a God, doesn't it?"

It almost took his breath away. Not only was Bella Lark a beautiful creation herself, with her hair blowing in the wind and her blue eyes bright with appreciation, but he had never had any real conversations about faith and God with Gwen.

Sure, they had sat in church together on most Sundays and special occasions, but it had never spilled into their daily lives in any kind of significant way, and Bella's comment made him realize what he'd been missing.

They started walking again, and Bella fell a few steps behind, then Luke heard her give a sudden cry of surprise and pain.

He whirled to see that she had wrenched her foot in a divot and was teetering off-balance, with pain and fear of falling scrawled plainly on her face.

Thinking of nothing else, he turned back and rushed to her. He put his arm around her shoulders to steady her and reached down to help ease her foot out of the offending hole, making sure she had her balance and could walk.

Her eyes turned to him and clung, as her fingers gripped the arm that wasn't around her shoulders.

Her eyes seemed to be asking a question, but Luke had the strangest sensation that it was more a question for herself than for him.

They stood locked in that moment, unable to stop staring at each other, unable—or was it unwilling?—to relinquish the way they clung together. Feeling slightly dizzy, Luke wondered now if he was holding her up or she was holding him.

"What are you *doing*?" Lily's voice seemed at first to come from a great distance.

Then the sound of it and the repercussions of what it meant slammed full force into Luke. He stepped back, though still kept a steadying hand out for Bella in case she needed it, and watched the same realization dawn on her face.

They both turned and watched Lily struggle onto Hooligan's back.

"Lily, please wait…" Luke hurried toward them, while Bella flung a hand toward her mouth.

But whether it was Lily's inexperience that triggered it or his and Bella's distress, Hooligan was off like a shot almost before Lily was properly in the saddle.

Chapter Ten

Inwardly fuming at Luke's carelessness, Bella called to her daughter and sprinted after her and the horse in a futile attempt to catch up with them.

If anything happened to Lily, she wouldn't let him forget it. But then another horse, a beauty with a sable coat and proud head, charged out of the barn with Luke riding him, and Bella watched clutching her heart and breathing prayers while they caught up with Lily and Hooligan and Luke was able to ease them to a stop.

Lily slid off the horse with her face flamed with a red that seemed more caused by embarrassment than fear. She stalked away, past Luke and her mother, back toward their cabin.

Bella nodded in Luke's direction and mouthed, "Thank you."

He nodded back, and it wasn't until she saw his weary, utterly relieved look that she remembered his apprehension around horses and realized what it must have taken for him to do what he'd done.

As she followed Lily back to their cabin, she regretted the fact that she'd immediately been ready to blame him.

It was easier to blame Luke than to blame herself, but that had never been her style.

She'd chosen a life of independence rather than risk being

betrayed and assaulted by another man and had always taken responsibility for her own decisions and actions.

Except now she had no idea why she hadn't protested more when Lily said she wanted to ride Hooligan. Part of it, she knew, was because Lily was already so upset with her over her refusal to talk about who her father was, and she had welcomed the opportunity to appease her.

But another part—the part that was hardest to face—was her intrigue with a certain handsome ranch owner. She experienced no fear or repulsion with him. She trusted him implicitly with her daughter.

She liked him. It was as simple as that.

But that wasn't at all what this summer was supposed to be about, and now Lily, who the summer *was* supposed to be about, had grown disenchanted.

Bella had offered her skills to help New Hope spring to life again, but so far there hadn't been any real follow through. Despite efforts she'd made to discuss the matter with Luke, she could tell his heart wasn't prepared for changes. So, if her daughter wasn't enjoying herself here, then what was the point of staying?

Maybe it really would be best if they went home.

The fact that the immediate thought that followed was how difficult it would be to tell Luke this, how she already ached picturing his determined smile, coupled with his wounded eyes, told her that it was exactly the right decision to make.

She entered the cabin with caution. Lily sat in one of the chairs in the room, thumbing through a magazine.

The tension that had been in the air had collapsed into the kind of retreat that meant that Lily didn't have the emotional energy for a fight anymore, but still wasn't willing for things to get back to normal.

Maybe things would never be "normal" again.

As Lily got older, it was a sure thing that she'd have more questions about who her father was, not fewer.

Please help me, Lord. Help me to know what to say, what to do.

She was preparing herself to break the news to Lily that she'd decided they should cut their visit short, when her phone rang.

It was Felicity Bond.

Bella heaved a frustrated sigh. She wasn't even surprised that her boss had proven herself unable to keep her promise to give her some space.

"Hello, Felicity," she said briskly into the phone.

Lily looked up from her magazine and rolled her eyes, which Bella chose to take as a sign of solidarity.

"Just checking in," Felicity said, in a very Felicity-like way, which meant bulldozing over any acknowledgment that she wasn't honoring their agreement.

"Jeb is getting anxious for your answer," she said. "He's not a patient man, and there are many others who would be eager to take him on as a client."

Normally, these words would have caused Bella a significant level of stress as she was usually determined to prove that she could handle any assignment.

But such a cloak of peace and of certainty came over her that she had no doubt what her response was meant to be.

"Please give the assignment to someone else," she said. "I told you that I don't want to work with Jeb Martin, and I haven't changed my mind about that."

No doubt shock had propelled Felicity into a rare silence, and Bella savored the few seconds it lasted.

"I want to make sure you fully understand the repercussions of making this choice," Felicity said in a dangerously calm voice.

"Yes, I understand," Bella said, though now that the elation was over and the reality of being unemployed faced her, an inner quaking began, and she was only able to keep a neutral voice and expression by focusing on Lily, who had discarded the magazine and was listening intently: Lily, her daughter who she was responsible to provide for.

A powerful urge to reverse her decision almost had Bella wanting to take back her words, apologize and say that she would work with Jeb after all.

But then she pictured him smiling like a man who always got his way, or at least fully believed that he deserved to.

She knew that kind of smile all too well.

"I understand my decision," she said in a firm voice. "And I stand by it."

"I'll expect you to email me by tomorrow morning your intent to resign," Felicity said. She didn't add anything about Bella having been a valuable employee or being sorry to lose her, but then again, that would have been expecting something her boss wasn't capable of.

Felicity always had been and always would be all about what she thought was best for the business.

"We'll iron out the formalities when you are back from your holiday," she added and ended the call.

"What did your boss want?" Lily asked, while Bella clutched the phone against her chest, heart racing.

She considered making something up but then was reminded of the promise she'd made to herself long ago that, since she was keeping the horrible circumstances of her birth from Lily, she would always be as open as she could about other things.

Besides, she would welcome any opportunity to distract Lily from asking questions about her father.

"She wanted to talk about my job," she said. She took a

deep breath. "I won't be working for her anymore. But we'll be okay," she hurried on to say. "I have some savings, and I have years of experience… I'll find another job in no time."

She added a silent prayer that would prove to be true.

She looked at Lily, trying to gauge her reaction.

"I never liked Felicity," Lily said. She got up. "Can I go see what Alison is doing?"

Is that it?

Bella didn't know whether to be relieved or hurt that her daughter was so casual about her mother's sudden unemployment. Then she gathered herself, realizing that, of course, Lily was still a child for the most part, and it was exactly the right thing for a child to be able to believe that if a parent said everything would be okay, it would be.

It caused Bella to reflect briefly on her relationship with her Heavenly Father. The Bible promised that God was always with her, but she sometimes still wondered where He had been that night or why He had allowed it to happen.

But she clung to her faith because it didn't make things any better—and probably would make them worse—to give it up. Someday she might understand the reason.

Maybe.

She gave Lily permission to go up to the house.

At the door of the cabin, Lily turned. "Can you tell Luke I'm sorry?" she said all in a rush. "And can I please try riding again? I promise I'll be more careful."

Yes, Hooligan had been startled and had taken off without Lily's command but it had still been her daughter's intention to escape.

The reason for that, at least what she assumed was the reason, caused an unfamiliar warmth to sweep through Bella, and she could feel her cheeks grow hot.

But then again, had she only imagined that Lily had ridden off because she was upset at what she'd seen? Whatever the situation was, she wasn't asking questions about it now.

Or, Bella wondered, was her daughter picking up her habit of avoiding the things that were too difficult to talk about?

It can't be any other way, she argued with herself, *not when it comes to* him.

With Lily gone, Bella no longer had to keep her emotions at bay. The problem was, she didn't know exactly how she felt about what had transpired.

She paced the cabin restlessly, picking up the magazine that Lily had been reading—one about championship horses—and set it down again. She caught a glimpse of her reflection in the mirror that hung over the dresser: her eyes anxious, her mouth set in a firm line.

It wasn't that she doubted her decision, if she could call it a decision when her back had been pushed against the figurative wall. But, despite what she'd said to Lily, she wasn't at all sure what she was going to do regarding employment. She worked in a highly competitive business, and reputations could be won or lost in an instant.

She already knew that Felicity would not handle her reputation with care.

With a sudden urge to talk to another adult about what had transpired, Bella pulled her phone out of her pocket and tried calling her friend Emery, but the call went directly to voice mail.

It was almost a relief. Emery was a good friend, energetic and always sure of her choices and opinions. She was also unerringly practical. These could all be good things on many occasions, but right now Bella needed someone who could at least try to understand why she'd made her decision and give her some hope for the future, not someone who would tell her she'd made a bad choice.

Luke. I want to talk to Luke.

She just wouldn't think about the way he was looking at her before Lily rode off on Hooligan.

She definitely wouldn't think about how she'd had a thought she hadn't allowed herself, or even wanted, to have in so long:

What would it be like to kiss him?

Luke had led the horse he'd rode, a deep brown beauty named Sire, and Hooligan back into the stables. He apologized to both of them for their brief excursions and promised they would get more attention and exercise later.

The interesting thing he'd discovered was that in having to display confidence around the horses for the sake of his guests, some of his own fear had evaporated.

Or maybe God was finally coming through for him. It would be nice to be able to think so.

What he knew for sure was that he would have jumped onto the nearest horse—or into a racing car or anything that moved—if doing so could erase the fear from Bella's face.

"You guys aren't so bad," he said, walking up and down the stables, doling out caresses here and there. "How about I bring you some treats later, how would that be?"

Some appeared to listen attentively, while others were preoccupied, flicking their tails at flies, gnawing at their feed.

None of them were monsters.

Luke knew this but also knew that other fears, not concrete but as real as the noble beasts around him, continued to loom.

"Would you happen to have any treats handy for me?"

Bella's plaintive voice behind him should have startled him, but somehow it didn't. Of course he'd expected that at some point she would track him down so they could debrief on what had happened.

Will we talk just about how Lily took off or how it seemed for a moment there like we were almost going to kiss?

Luke gave the horse nearest him one last pat and turned to her. As he did so, he registered her question about the treats. That was a strange way to start a conversation, whether she wanted to talk about girls on runaway horses or a potential kiss.

He studied Bella's face. He couldn't guess what she was thinking about, but he was sure it wasn't either of those things.

"Let's go talk somewhere." It wasn't even a question, and she nodded.

"Lily is up at the house with Alison," Bella said, letting him know it wouldn't be the best place for whatever conversation she wanted to have.

"Can I take you to one of my favorite places?" he asked. "It's only a short drive away, and it's quiet enough so we can talk, but there are always people around too."

Bella darted him a look that told him that she both appreciated his understanding but was also a little put off by it.

He wondered then if he could read her in a way that others couldn't. He could picture her at work, all efficiency and briskness and smiles that didn't quite reach her eyes, and he concluded that maybe, for some reason, he did have some insight.

Or maybe, looking at the way her hair tumbled around her shoulders, he just wanted to think that he did.

"I do a lot of thinking there," Luke added, wondering while he gave his sales pitch why he was sharing his favorite spots with this woman—first Jacob's café and now the small, hidden gem of a chapel—when he knew she could leave at any moment.

It would be August before they knew it, and the air and the daylight would do that thing that had left him with a wistful, undefinable longing ever since he was a boy, knowing that though new beginnings were coming, there were going to be things left behind that he could never get back.

"I'll just message Lily and let her know I'll be gone for a little while in case she's looking for me." Her thumbs danced over her phone and then she watched for the answer. "She might not want me to go."

No doubt, she was still thinking of the way Lily had ridden off, and Luke wanted to ask her if they'd talked about... whatever it was.

He wasn't sure himself.

But then a ping signaled a reply, and Bella read it and gave a brief nod.

"Okay," she said. "Where are we going?"

Luke explained their destination as they walked to his vehicle. From what he knew of Bella, she would not be one for the "oh you'll see when we get there" school of thought.

"There's small chapel not far from here," he said. "It only sits about fifty people at the most, but they still hold one service on Sundays. It's kind of a word-of-mouth situation, and sometimes there might be a full house, but other times maybe only five or ten people. But..." He paused, trying to give adequate words to his feelings. "I feel God's presence there. Always, no matter what I'm going through."

Bella nodded, getting into the passenger side of the car and buckling up her seat belt.

"Will there be a service this Sunday?" she asked.

"Yes, I think so."

She nodded again.

For a few minutes, they drove in silence, then Luke said, "There are always a few people around other days of the week, mostly volunteers, to make sure the lawn gets mowed, clear snow in the winter and check on the building, that kind of thing."

As Luke had promised, it was only a short distance from

the ranch, but if he hadn't known what he was looking for, it would have been easy to drive by the nondescript building nestled in between bushes a little ways down a rugged, slightly winding path.

He eased the car to a stop in an unattended parking lot near the top of the path.

Bella looked at him questioningly.

"It's just down there." He pointed.

She looked and located the small building.

"The path isn't steep," he said as they got out of the car. "But if you need me, just grab on."

The words hovered in the air, weighed down with potential meaning.

"I'll be fine," Bella said with her customary briskness. As if to prove it, she hurried ahead of him and led the way down the path. He stayed close behind her. While the path wasn't steep, there were loose pieces of rock that could upset one's balance.

She arrived at the bottom safely though and threw a triumphant glance over her shoulder.

Why does she have so much to prove? Luke wondered.

Just as he'd said, a young woman was there mowing the lawn. She was tall, dressed in blue-jean shorts and a tank top and had an eagle tattooed on her right shoulder.

She stopped as they passed by, pushed her bangs away from her sweating forehead and waved at them.

They waved back, and Bella asked, "Do you know her?"

Luke shook his head. "No, first time I've seen her. The volunteers are like that. Word gets out, and they decide it's a cool thing to tend to this little church in the woods, like it's their good deed for the day or something. But often it's a one-off, and only a few of them who are willing to tend the grounds will come back for the service."

"Who's the pastor here?" Bella asked. "Doesn't it get discouraging?"

"The pastors change too," Luke said. "It really depends on who is close by and who has time to do it. Sometimes, someone will come out from Trydale or a nearby town, and there's a few that circulate between the church camps in the surrounding areas that will take their turn. I don't think it's discouraging for them," he added. "I've heard some say that they feel close to God here too, like it isn't so much about how many people are there as it is about being sure that He is listening."

Bella listened, her head tilted to one side, absorbing his words.

"Would you like to see the inside?" Luke asked.

Sharing this was particularly impactful because he had never taken Gwen to this chapel while they were dating, never would have even considered it. Gwen liked churches that had pews filled from end to end with well-dressed people and featured huge, expertly trained worship teams and television-ready pastors.

Going to church with Gwen had always been an empty experience, Luke now realized. He didn't just want to show up to be seen. He wanted someone with whom he could discuss what they'd learned.

That was if he was looking for someone, but there were too many pressing matters in his life for that.

Still, he couldn't help speculating that if Bella and he lived in the same place, or if she was going to stay beyond the summer, they could become real friends.

The wood of the small chapel door had warped a bit with all the rain, and Luke had to give it a good yank to get it to open. When it did, the familiar scent of pine and earthiness rushed out at him. On Sundays, this scent would be mingled with the candles that were lit and sometimes with flowers, if anyone had donated some for the altar.

He watched Bella taking it all in, instinctively breathing in the atmosphere of the place the way he did.

There was nothing in the least ornate about it. The walls were plain, other than a few obviously handcrafted wall-hangings that adorned them. The long benches were not built for comfort, and the cross on the wall behind the pulpit looked like it had been fashioned out of ancient wood.

Luke almost instantly experienced the profound peace that washed over him in this place. He prayed that Bella would find the same.

An elderly man was sweeping out debris from one of the corners near the back of the chapel. When he saw them, he made a sort of tipping his hat motion and picked up his broom.

"Don't let us interrupt you," Luke said, but the man smiled and said, "I can always tell when someone needs time here."

His eyes were on Bella when he said it, and Luke was glad that her head was turned the other way, studying one of the wall hangings. The colors were eye-catching, though the figures in it—a group of men lifting a large net of fish out of the water—were almost stick-like.

The sweeper left, and Luke asked Bella if she wanted to sit for a little while.

She hesitated but then lowered herself onto the back bench and slid over to make room for him. He sat beside her, careful not to crowd her space.

They sat in silence for a couple of minutes then she turned to him and said words that he wouldn't have guessed if he'd been given a hundred guesses.

"I quit my job. I really didn't have a choice."

He turned to face her, trying not to show his shock because that was the last thing she needed to see. Her face wore an odd, anxious smile like she was somehow hoping herself that the words she'd said were just a badly delivered joke.

"Can I ask why?"

As briefly as possible, she told him about Jeb Martin and how she refused to promote his shady agenda.

"My boss has made it clear that making money is more important to her than being loyal to me," she finished.

"That's not right," Luke protested, surprising himself with how angry and protective he felt on her behalf. "There must be something you can do. Would you consider taking your employer to court?"

"I don't know." She shrugged, her face soft and troubled.

He wondered if she knew how beautiful she was when her guard was down, then scolded himself for making that observation under the circumstances.

"In some ways," she continued, "it's kind of a relief... I mean other than the being an unemployed single mom part." She gave a sad laugh that snapped off in the middle, and he watched her swallow hard.

He hesitated, not knowing if he should reach out to comfort her, but then she got a grip on herself and said, "It was going to be hanging over my head all summer. I was supposed to spend the time making the decision on whether I was willing to take Jeb on as a client. I knew I was never going to be willing, so why drag out the inevitable?"

A slight tremor in her hands belied the practicality with which she spoke the words.

"You must have a loyal client base, right?" Luke said, his mind turning with ideas, even as another part of him knew that he did not have the time to solve someone else's problems and that it was ridiculous to try when he hadn't come up with a clear solution for his own.

But we could help each other.

The thought came to him like an answer to a prayer he hadn't known how to put into words. Bella had already expressed her interest in bringing more publicity to the ranch and had expressed every confidence that she could do so. What if New Hope officially became her new client, and he let people know that? Of course she would have to be paid, which he couldn't really afford...

He almost growled in frustration but refused to give up the idea that there must be an answer—for both of them.

"Bella?" Luke realized what he was about to ask, but there was no going back now, and he trusted it was the right thing to do. "Can I pray for you?"

Surprised flared in her lovely blue eyes, but she nodded.

Usually when he prayed with others, they would join hands. He had no such expectation of Bella and so experienced his own flare of surprise—plus something he couldn't name— when she reached out and took his hand.

Her touch caused him to momentarily lose his voice and shattered his concentration before he recovered himself.

"Dear Lord. You know what Bella's needs are. You know her gifts. You know she has a daughter to care for. Please help her to trust in You, to trust that there is a solution to her current problem and that You will help her find it soon. I pray this in Your Son's name. Amen."

Bella said, "Amen," and withdrew her hands from his. It was like the absence of something he didn't know he was missing.

"I didn't mean to eavesdrop..."

They both turned to see the man with the broom.

"But please know that I will be praying too for whatever your needs are."

"Thank you," Bella said quietly, though Luke could sense

her closing off slightly, unsure whether to consider this a kindness or an intrusion.

The man leaned the broom he'd been using against the wall and approached them with his hand extended. "Pastor Stewart Benson," he introduced himself.

"Luke Duffy," Luke said, offering his hand, "and this is Bella Lark."

Bella also shook his hand.

"Do you folks live around here?" he asked.

"My family owns New Hope Ranch," Luke said. "Not far from here. Bella and her daughter are guests for the summer."

"That's great to hear," Pastor Stewart said. "I hope you can join me here for church on Sunday."

"Where's your home church, if you don't mind me asking?" Luke said.

"Right here, I hope." The pastor's grin widened, taking years off of his rugged face, despite the white hair on his head. "I'm hoping and praying I can get the word out."

Get the word out...

Luke slid a look Bella's way, wondering if she was thinking the same thing that he was.

First the ranch needed more exposure and now someone was looking to bring new life to the chapel too.

Was God trying to tell them something?

He had a twinge of regret that the hidden gem of a chapel might soon be something that he had to share with more people, but the look of hope in Bella's eyes soon chased that feeling away.

Chapter Eleven

"I actually happen to be in public relations and marketing," Bella told Pastor Stewart. She dug around in her purse and pulled out a business card to give to him.

The pastor studied her card.

"She's helping with PR for the ranch too," Luke said.

"Not really that much yet," Bella interjected. The last thing she wanted to do was mislead anyone. She'd just left her job because she was determined not to do that.

"But I am good at what I do," she added, as much for Luke's benefit as for the pastor's. "I'm good at seeing what places need done to bring out their full potential."

"I'm sure you are," Pastor Stewart said. He offered her card back to her. "But I'm afraid I don't have the budget to hire a professional public relations person."

"Keep my card," Bella urged. "And if you have time after church on Sunday, maybe you can tell me what brought you here and why you want this to be your home church."

"I'd like that very much," the pastor said warmly.

On the drive back to the ranch Bella asked, "So what were you doing back there?"

"I'm not sure what you're referring to," Luke said, keeping his eyes carefully on the road, which led her to think that he knew exactly what she was talking about.

"Making it sound to the pastor like you and I have been on the same page about the ranch."

Luke shrugged slightly. "I guess I want you to have as many doors open to you as possible, even if I am still having my own struggles, you were put in an unfair position."

"But it's not your place to fix it."

Luke sighed, easing the car into a turn toward the highway that would take them back to New Hope.

"If we're going to be honest about that, it's not your place to fix the ranch either."

Okay, he had a point.

"Would it be completely out of line," Luke said, his eyes back on the road, "to say that we're just two people who want to help each other?"

It wasn't an unreasonable question or an unreasonable idea. Luke would have no way of knowing how deep and tangled the roots of her lack of trust were…or why.

But maybe it was time for her to get over it?

No, no, that was wrong. It was not the kind of thing she would ever get over. But did she have to let it hang over her entire life, coloring everything in harsh, angry strokes far outside the lines of what she would have wished for her life?

She turned her head and took in Luke's strong-jawed profile. She considered the way he drove, confidently but never recklessly, the care he took with Lily, the way he always looked people in the eyes when he talked to them.

If she was asked if she trusted him, she realized that her answer would be yes.

"It's not out of line," she answered.

"Whew," Luke said. "You had me worried there."

"I'm not…" Bella began and stopped.

"You're not what?" Luke encouraged her to continue.

Not used to trusting people. Not used to counting on any-one but myself.

"…I'm not sure what I want to work on first."

By the early weeks of August, Bella and Luke had settled into a kind of give-and-take routine that she found surprisingly enjoyable.

She had been so used to viewing the end of summer as an unwanted, looming deadline for her to make a decision about her job that it was almost a relief that the decision had been made.

Of course, there was still the matter of Lily returning to school in September. With everything else jostling around in her mind and wanting to focus on Lily having an enjoyable summer, Bella had shoved that to the back of her mind.

Would Lily return to the same school and, if so, would she break out of her shell?

She was fine at the ranch—she was *great* at the ranch. It was as if she and Hooligan had been bonded for years, her confidence with the horse grew daily, and Bella could see how that confidence was spilling over into other areas of her life. Her friendship with Alison continued to grow, and Bella no longer worried about the young teen having a detrimental impact on her daughter. Instead, she could see ways that the young girls encouraged and helped one another.

Once again, Lily's attention to detail and sensitivity to the people around her had proven itself: she had been sure that Alison's behavior was driven by emotional pain, and she was right.

But the ranch wasn't home, and when they did get home would all the same problems return? That question coupled with the knowledge that she didn't have a job to go back to twisted Bella's stomach.

If she could stay focused, then maybe the biggest and worst

question of all wouldn't continue to plague her: how long would it be before Lily's questions about her father surfaced again and grew more persistent? Because Bella knew there was no way they were going to go away.

It was midweek, and Bella was in the kitchen pouring herself a cup of coffee. For the moment, she was alone. Lily and Alison had gone out to the stables to visit the horses, and at breakfast, Nora had mentioned that she had errands in town, being a bit vague about the details.

"I could take you, Mom," Luke offered. "I just have a few things to take care of this morning, but that shouldn't take long."

"That's all right, Luke," Nora said. "Cal said he has to go in for something himself and is happy to take me."

Tension pulsed and Bella could see that Luke was filled to the brim with questions and protests but tamping them down because of others at the table.

She was tempted to find a reason for her, Lily and Alison to excuse themselves so that Luke and Nora could have it out.

Bella wasn't too keen herself on Nora going into town with Cal, but it wasn't really her concern.

Before the air in the room could grow any thicker, Nora said, "Oh, look at the time. I'd better get ready to go."

Now, Bella took a pondering sip of her coffee, looking out the kitchen window. It struck her how much she would miss this view when it was time to return home.

Is that the only thing I'm going to miss?

As if to answer her own question, her pulse quickened when Luke strolled into the kitchen. He wore the shadow of what had happened at breakfast on his face, but when he saw her, his expression altered, softened, and Bella wondered if he was getting used to having her around as much as she was getting used to being around him.

"Ready to visit the fishing pond?" he asked her and then chuckled as her face crinkled reflexively in distaste.

"You don't have to fish, city girl," he said teasingly. "I just want to show you where it is. It's a pretty spot."

Since they had both committed to working together in a genuine way—with Bella helping Luke find ways to more effectively promote what the ranch had to offer, while adding this to her resume of successes for when she was tackling the job market again—Luke had chosen a different spot each morning for them to visit before he resumed training with Lily and Hooligan.

"Though, I bet you'd look cute in a pair of hip waders," he added.

Bella's heart jolted, but she remained silent so long that Luke looked embarrassed.

"I'm sorry," he said. "That wasn't very professional of me."

"It's fine," she said, and her mouth pulled in a tight smile.

She liked Luke, she really did. She felt more at ease in his presence than she'd ever expected to feel around any man ever again. He had something about him that radiated both strength and gentleness; she liked his direct gaze and couldn't help appreciating his strong jaw and how at ease he was in his own body. She also deeply admired the way he worked to put his own fears aside for the good of others.

But she wasn't ready to have him flirt with her, if that was what he was trying to do, and she would never be ready to flirt back.

I flirted that night; I know I did.

Luke quietly cleared this throat, and Bella pulled herself back into the present moment.

"We don't have to go to the pond," he said. "Is there something else you'd rather do?"

"No, let's go," she said. Luke still looked uncertain, so she added, "I really want to see it."

Bella noticed as they walked that he kept a careful distance between them. It wasn't that they'd ever held hands or he'd draped an arm around her shoulder, but sometimes their arms or shoulders would brush as they walked together and talked about various things.

Now the space between them felt wide and full of unanswered questions, and the silence between them wasn't exactly a comfortable one.

Bella was used to the walls she'd erected to protect herself since that night. Her life was full and about as busy as she wanted it to be with the juggling act of being a single mother and having a successful career. But now that career was in limbo, Lily was growing up and, for the first time, she let herself consider how keeping those walls up could not only keep bad things out but also potentially good things too.

"Have you ever ridden?" Luke asked, still looking ahead as he walked beside—but apart—from her.

At first, Bella was so relieved that he had broken the silence that it didn't fully register what he'd asked.

"Ridden?" She pulled the trick of repeating the last word she'd heard.

"Horses," Luke said, a note of drollness finding its way back into his voice. "You've been here on a ranch for over a month now, and I just realized that we've never talked about that."

"Just ponies at the Exhibition," Bella said. "But that was years ago. To be honest, I don't know where Lily gets her interest from."

She tensed and inwardly prayed that Luke wouldn't suggest it came from her father.

He didn't but did say thoughtfully, "We may have to rectify that." He stopped walking, so Bella stopped too.

"Would you be interested in going on a trail ride some time? Lily and Alison too," he added hastily. "I used to lead trail rides if no one else was available. It usually wasn't too bad because the horses tended to be sedate and knew the routes well. I've realized lately that I kind of miss it, and maybe it's something I could start promoting more."

Bella wasn't sure how keen she was on the idea of riding, but she was happy that whatever door she was afraid she'd permanently closed was being cracked open again.

She would never want more from Luke than friendship, but she did want that. It surprised her how much.

"I'll definitely consider it, but I'm sure Lily would just about fall off her horse at the sight of me."

They laughed together, and Bella's heart opened slightly more, like a slow blossoming flower not ready to be in full bloom but finding more light than she ever thought it would.

In some ways, though, it was still almost too much. She wasn't used to this lightness, this slightly giddy feeling of having fun with a man. She had the need to ground herself so she did what she often did when other things were too over-whelming to think about and returned her thoughts to work.

"I'm still thinking about Pastor Stewart and the chapel," she mused.

She saw Luke's face make the adjustment to the change in subject.

"Okay…" he said.

"With it being so close to the ranch, I'm wondering if there's anything I could come up with to help bring attention to both of them."

Right now, Bella wasn't even particularly thinking about the fact that neither of these clients—if you could call them that—could pay her. Being of a cautious nature, always hav-ing money set aside for emergencies came naturally to her, so she had enough savings to carry them through at least a few months, and she did trust that if she remained diligent, God would meet her halfway.

Her deeper urge was to truly help causes she believed in.

"Interesting thought," Luke said. "What did you have in mind?"

"I'm not exactly sure yet," Bella said. "But I'll keep you posted."

Luke nodded. "Whatever you come up with, I know it will be great."

She'd never before had a partner with whom she wanted to share ideas.

This time, when the giddiness came, she let it.

Luke enjoyed watching Bella take in what was commonly referred to as the fishing hole, a modest description that didn't begin to do justice to the wide, clear pond under trees that provided the perfect amount of shade and surrounded by gently rolling hills adorned with wildflowers.

Oh, who was he kidding? He always liked watching her.

Right now, her eyes took in her surroundings with an appreciative, almost reverent look. She sighed and turned her face up to the sky, breathing deeply. Then, just as he was about to find the courage to tell her how beautiful he found her, she pulled out the notebook she always carried with her and began to jot things down.

"Maybe at the chapel, there could be a sign telling people about the fishing here," she mused as she made notes. "And for when people were here, we could put signs up or let them know in some way about the chapel."

"We still need money," Luke said, hating to discourage her creative flow, but sometimes it seemed like she was forgetting she wasn't getting paid for any of this. He couldn't live with himself if there was even a hint that he was taking advantage of her.

"I know," she said, glancing his way. "Later today, I plan to finish up the list of clients I've bonded with in the past and start reaching out to them."

Luke shook his head. "I still wish I was giving you a better holiday."

An almost shy expression crossed Bella's face, different from her usual retreat into a defensive self-protection, even though she said, "It's not up to you."

"Well, I think it kind of is," Luke said, "since you are paying guests at the ranch." But even as he said it, he was aware they both knew that Bella had never been just a regular guest. She'd always been too aware of what was going on and determined to do something about it.

"Next time, we'll bring the fishing gear," he said, mostly to see her reaction. But he had a sudden vision of him teaching Bella how to bait a hook, gently guiding her hands, and suddenly what was meant to tease her almost captured his breath.

But she said, "Maybe we should." Then she gave him a look that told him that she knew what he was doing.

"Knowing you," Luke said with a laughing shrug of surrender, "you'll turn out to be a better fisherman than I ever was."

"Fisherperson," she corrected him with a saucy tilt to her head.

"I should probably get back to the stables," Luke said, fighting to keep reluctance from his voice. He didn't want Bella to think that he didn't look forward to the time he spent with Lily because that wasn't true in the least. On the contrary, it was a joy and honor to see what an affinity Lily had for the horses and to watch the bond between her and Hooligan grow daily.

It was just that whenever he spent time with Bella, an emotion that had been buried ever since Gwen chose Brett over him started to bubble to the surface. At first, he thought it meant he was feeling something that he hadn't felt for a long time. Then, he realized that it was something he had never felt.

Gwen had never brought out in him this strange, heady mixture of both wanting to protect and learn from someone. Bella was fragile and strong, vulnerable and tough as nails.

"Yes, I guess it's about that time," Bella said.

Was it wishful thinking or did he hear reluctance in her voice?

But he couldn't dwell on that. Despite what—if anything—might be happening between them, he had a job to do.

"Has your daughter ever considered a career in horse training?" Luke speculated as they headed toward the stables. "She'd be a natural."

Bella's eyes widened in surprise, but then her face softened at the compliment.

"She is doing really well here. I wish…" Her voice trailed wistfully away.

"What do you wish?" Luke urged.

"I wish that I knew it would last."

"I wish that too," Luke said, and he could feel her eyes on him, filled with questions that he wasn't sure he'd be able to answer.

They do have a school in town, he thought of saying but knew that neither of them were prepared for what that might imply.

Luke was beginning to wonder if he should be enrolling Alison for school in the fall. He seethed inwardly as he thought about the self-absorption being demonstrated by his brother and sister-in-law. They weren't easy to reach, being often out of cell phone range, and Brett's check-ins were sporadic at best.

There had been a few times when Luke wanted to ask his brother if he and Gwen even remembered that they had a daughter. He knew that wasn't totally fair or accurate. They really were decent parents in their own ways, and he supposed that they were probably heady with the sense of freedom and perhaps finding new life in their relationship.

But still…

"You're quiet," Bella observed, touching his wrist lightly and fleetingly. She'd developed a habit of doing that, punctuating her thoughts or encouraging him to share his. Luke wasn't even sure that she knew she was doing it. What he did know each time it happened was the sensation of being fully present and aware. So, for a second, when she asked him what he had been thinking about, he couldn't remember that he'd been thinking of anyone but her.

"Just thinking about the new school year being here before long," Luke said. He had developed the habit of answering her questions without trying to put a spin on anything, having realized how comforting it was to have someone to talk openly to. "I'm starting to think I'm going to have to enroll Alison in town."

"What's the school in town like?" Bella asked with a pensive look on her face.

"It was a decent school when I went," Luke said. "But that was a long time ago."

"School's coming up soon for Lily too," Bella mused, half talking to herself. "The time's gone too fast."

Luke wondered what the right thing to say was.

But then she was changing the subject, asking, "What kind of errand do you think your mother had to run in town that she'd asked Cal to drive her?"

Luke's stomach clenched.

"I don't really know, but I'm afraid of what I think I know. I think she might have gone to the bank."

Bella nodded, concern furrowing her forehead, but they

were at the stables, and Lily and Alison were laughing together, making a show of waving their arms in the air like controllers on a runway bringing an airplane in to land.

"This place has been so good for her," Bella murmured, reaching out to briefly press his hand. "I have you to thank for that."

Luke's heart stuttered with startled joy, but he saw Lily's and Alison's eyes tracking and thought it was just as well that the contact was brief.

"What do you want to do today?" he asked Lily, striding forward.

"Ride, of course," she said. "Can Alison go with me?"

The phrasing of the question didn't escape Luke. Not "Can she come with us?"

Alison was doing better than he'd expected after the rocky start to their summer, and he was glad the girls were friends. But that didn't mean he was ready to let them ride off together without supervision. He could too easily imagine Alison encouraging Lily to take risks or the two of them simply getting distracted by their chatter and giggles.

"We'll all go." He made sure the girls knew it wasn't optional.

"I guess so," Lily said with a glance in Alison's direction.

"But what's Mom going to do?" she asked.

"She's welcome to come with us," Luke said.

"I don't think that's necessary," Bella hurried to say.

"Yeah," Lily agreed even more rapidly. "She's not even into horses. It wouldn't be fun for her, and she'd slow us down."

"I think," Luke said, focusing on Bella when he spoke and praying she would see his words as encouragement, "that your mother can do anything she sets her mind to, just like you can. In fact, I can see where you get it from."

He would never know whether it was his encouragement

or her daughter's discouragement—or maybe it was a combination of both—that prompted Bella to lift her chin and say that she would join them, but soon he was helping her onto a horse who was aptly named Serene and trained especially for trail rides.

You look beautiful up there. You look like you belong in my life.

Luke ordered his heart to simmer down. They both had lives to get back to. His mother was out on some mysterious errand with a man he trusted perhaps less than anyone he knew. Bella was unemployed and had to rectify that situation sooner rather than later.

But in that moment, when he saw her breathe deeply in and out, knowing that she was telling herself that she was capable, as the wind played in her hair the way his fingers longed to, his heart rebelliously refused to listen.

When Luke reminded himself that he was about to lead a trail ride and couldn't stay in a daydreaming bubble, he once again saw Lily taking notice, her expression unreadable.

"Is there any place you remember from your previous visits, Al?" he asked his niece, quelling his uneasiness. "That you'd like Lily and her mom to see?"

Lily and Alison exchanged looks, and he wondered suddenly what the girls had talked about in terms of comparing notes on their family situations.

"Wherever," Alison said.

"Okay," Luke said after a brief hesitation.

He guided his horse, Blaze, named so for the white mark on the forehead of the otherwise auburn horse, onto the beginner trail, and the others fell in behind.

He heard Bella try to start a conversation with Lily, but it didn't seem to be going far.

Once again, the practical part of him told him to back off

of…whatever it was he thought he was doing. The last thing he wanted was to cause or contribute in any way to a rift between mother and daughter, especially over what was basically like a schoolboy crush destined to go nowhere.

He watched as Alison rode up alongside him and then slightly ahead, indicating with a head gesture that Lily should catch up.

He tried to keep an eye on them while also making sure that Bella, looking regal on the sable beauty named Serene, was doing okay.

This would be a great time to have eyes in the back of my head.

"Hey, it looks like Grandma just got home," Alison remarked.

Luke automatically looked over his shoulder and caught a glimpse of Cal opening the passenger door and offering his hand to help Luke's mother out of the car.

The show of courtliness curdled his stomach.

"Do you want to go back?" Bella asked him, picking up on his thoughts as she often did.

He hesitated, looking back at the girls, who were now several paces ahead, urging their horses while, he suspected, trying to look like they weren't.

"Alison." He raised his voice slightly. "Lily, wait up please."

Their reluctance was in large print in their body language but they slowed and waited for him to catch up.

"Would you trust Alison to take you and Lily on a short ride?" he asked in a lowered tone.

Bella's brow furrowed. Then her face softened a little. "I know you must be anxious to get back and talk to your mom."

Luke nodded. "I am but it's not fair to Lily."

He could see Bella pondering, a thoughtful light in her lovely blue eyes.

"Okay, I'm asking this now as a serious question," she said. "Would you trust Alison?"

Luke could see Alison and Lily looking back at them now, confusion and impatience plain on their faces. He'd asked them to wait up, and now he was dawdling, talking to Bella.

He realized, with a pang of guilt, that he really hadn't given much thought to Alison, at least not to what she was really like as a person and what he remembered about her previous visits to the ranch. Of course, he was determined to live up to his responsibilities and make sure she was well taken care of as long as she was with them, but he'd had so much else on his mind that it had been guests to the ranch, not him, that noticed how she was acting out and were able to understand why.

Since Alison and Lily had become friends, Luke could see much more of the niece he remembered in Alison. She had always shared his kinship with the land—something her parents lacked—and she, like Lily, had an instinctive way with the horses.

"I would trust her," he was able to answer honestly. "I do trust her."

A decisive look came upon Bella's face.

"Then let's let the girls have a bit of a ride on their own, and I'll go back to the house with you."

Luke swallowed, overcome with something that he didn't quite recognize. "I can't ask you to do that."

"You didn't ask. I offered."

Was this what it would be like to have someone he could really count on?

Was this how it was to no longer feel alone in it all?

Chapter Twelve

What am I doing?

Bella wondered exactly when she had become the kind of mother who let her daughter go off riding with another adolescent while she went off to help a man.

Except, she knew, Luke wasn't just any man, and she could no longer dismiss him the way she had habitually done with others since that fateful night.

For one thing, she trusted him, something she considered a gift from God because she hadn't thought she would ever be able to do that. For another thing, she actually *liked* him, though she still held on to the idea that she would never act on that. She still believed that, ultimately, she was meant to do life on her own.

The look of surprise and gratitude on Lily's face helped to push away at least some of Bella's second-guessing herself.

"Really, Mom? You'll let me go riding with Al, just us?"

"As long as you promise not to go far and to be careful."

Luke affirmed the instructions, and the girls nodded enthusiastically.

An unexpected rush of relief coursed through Bella as she watched them ride away, chattering excitedly. Maybe the relief came from being apprehensive that Lily's excitement might soon turn to skepticism. She was, Bella knew, still keeping an eye on her mother's interactions with the handsome ranch owner, and Bella uneasily wondered if Lily would think she had ulterior motives for giving permission for the unsupervised ride.

Do I have ulterior motives?

Bella asked the question of herself then turned it into a prayer, asking that her Heavenly Father keep her from making unwise decisions.

Yet when she thought about Luke, all she ever experienced was a sense of peace and an urge to know him better…and to be the person who could help alleviate some of the pressures in his life.

Only because it gives me more experience and will help me get a new job, she attempted to remind herself.

There was another reason for giving the unexpected permission too, and Bella wasn't proud of it, but she really hoped to deter Lily from her increasing questions about her father.

"What's wrong?" Luke asked, homing in on her with concern in his eyes, and Bella realized she must have grimaced.

"Are you worried about the girls?" he continued. "You know I didn't expect you to come with me. I wouldn't be surprised if my mother doesn't have much to say. She hasn't been very forthcoming these days."

Bella could see the shadow come into his eyes and knew it pained him to speak out against his mother, even if what he was saying was true.

"I wanted to come," she said. "I'm hoping I can remind your mother not to make any hasty decisions. She did promise that she wouldn't do anything until I had a chance to think about what kind of marketing could be done here. Besides, it's good for Lily and me for me to give her some more independence."

Luke exhaled a breath, his expression troubled, and for a moment, Bella was worried that he knew what she was thinking.

"I think we're already past how much time my mother said

she would give you," he said. "That is, if she even kept the promise in mind."

They stood at the front door. "After you," Luke said, opening the door. Bella went in ahead of him. She paused for a moment, using a trick she employed sometimes to put herself in the headspace of seeing something with fresh eyes.

The sun streamed in through the windows. The light did show places on the walls that needed paint touch-ups, scuffs on the hardwood floors and faded patches on the carpet. But it also showed the artistry of the craftsmanship in the furniture, tables and shelves, the beloved history of the place in landscape paintings and family photos and something intangible, a sense of comfort and welcome that said that this place had stories to tell and would welcome the stories of others to add to its history.

A bed and breakfast...

"A bed and breakfast," she exclaimed out loud to Luke. "You need to turn this place into a full-fledged bed and breakfast."

Now that they were inside, he had removed his hat, and his hair had that tousled look that Bella realized she had grown fond of. It made her fingers itch to reach out and brush the strands of hair out of his eyes...

What? I never think things like that.

"Ummm," Luke said with a puzzled frown, "isn't that what we're already doing here? I mean it's just you and Lily, but we are providing beds and breakfast."

"No, I'm talking about going all in," Bella said, thinking out loud.

She could visualize it: guests not only around the kitchen table but also reading books and chatting about them in the library room, going for trail rides, recounting their days' adventures in the living room as they sipped tea and ate some cookies or maybe fresh fruit in the evenings.

"I'm talking about having people stay in the house. Of course," she mused, "you'd still have the cabin we're in for overflow."

"Overflow," Luke repeated in a flat tone. "You're talking about overflow."

"I know it sounds like a longshot," Bella said, tugging at his hands a little, hardly even realizing she was doing it. "But sometimes these ideas come into my head that I'm so sure about, and Luke, I have a gut feeling in spades about this one. Besides, remember we always need a horizon goal."

"I'm glad you're so enthusiastic," Luke said, and she noticed that he was squeezing her hands back. Actually, they were standing there holding hands like it was the most natural thing in the world.

She almost forgot what they were talking about until Luke continued, "But I'm not getting what the new idea is. It's pretty much what we're already doing, isn't it?"

"In a way, yes," Bella let go of Luke's hands and headed toward the kitchen, looking over her shoulder, not so much to assure herself that Luke was following but because she trusted he would be.

I feel like I belong here.

She sat in a chair, charged with the same kind of energy she got when she was in a meeting with a client and knew she was about to bring something forward that would work for them.

"You're kind of doing that," she said. "But it needs to be a more immersive experience. You need to fully commit. Open this wonderful home up to people, let them be part of it, share its history. I just know it will make an enormous difference."

"That all sounds great," Luke said, still sounding unsure. "But I can't see my mother agreeing with any of this. At best,

she'll just want to get the ranch on the market as soon as possible or—" his face contorted as if he was in pain "—take the
Coopers' offer and sell it directly to them. At worst, she might
see it as a sign of disrespect to my father's legacy. Speaking
of my mother…" He stood up. "I did come in here to try to
find out why she went into town with Cal."

"I know," Bella said, standing too. "Would you let me talk
to her about my idea? I'm good at helping people see potential, even when they're sure there isn't any. It's what I do."

She knew she was coming across like this was another
business deal, and she could see by the way Luke was frown-
ing, almost like he had hurt feelings, that it sounded that way
to him too.

But it was just business, and she had to keep reminding
herself of that because, despite how at home she felt here and
how unexpectedly comfortable she was with Luke's touch, she
still had to face her own life at the end of the summer, which
now seemed to be hurtling toward her; she needed new clients,
she had to make a decision about Lily's future…

She'd never had the time or the heart for romantic dreams,
and she couldn't let herself start now.

Still, Luke was a friend—*Is that what he is?*—and for the
first time that Bella could remember, she wanted to stop hiding.

She wasn't ready to tell him everything. She would never
be ready for that, but maybe she could share something just
so he would know that the tentative bond they were forming
meant something to her too.

"I'm… I'm not the best at trusting people," she said slowly.

Luke looked slightly surprised at the non sequitur but then
nodded.

"I know I'm kind of bulldozing in here," Bella continued,
"talking about your beloved home like it's nothing but another

deal that I have make, and I *do* want it to be successful. But not just because I need a fresh start—because I want to help you to find one too. Does that make any sense at all?"

Bella looked at Luke's face, grave and attentive. She knew, or at least felt, that she was making a mess of what she was saying. It was still so difficult—almost impossible, it seemed—to talk about the things she didn't dare hope for: the things that, somewhere deep inside of her, she wondered if she could find with Luke.

"Can I ask you a question?" he said, his eyes steady on her face.

Bella swallowed and nodded.

"Does this lack of trust have anything to do with Lily's father?"

The question was a shockwave through her like a bolt from a stormy sky, although a part of her had expected it.

Her mouth was dry, and her heart hammered in her chest as she wondered how much she could say without bringing back the hideous sensations of that night.

A gray cloud of worry crossed into Luke's blue eyes.

"It looks like I shouldn't have asked," he said. "I'm sorry."

Bella closed her eyes and shook her head. "No," she managed to get out. "I know you didn't mean to upset me. It's natural you'd be curious."

She breathed slowly in and out, reminding herself that she wasn't back in that place with *him* and that God was with her.

So was the kind-hearted, sensitive rancher who daily faced his fears so that he could do his best to provide Bella and Lily with memorable days and who took on a parental role with a niece who had an attitude the size of this ranch.

"Lily's father," Bella said, "was not a good person."

The understatement almost made her laugh, and the unexpected jolt of humor helped her resist being pulled into a cave of dark memories.

"So, yes, he has a lot to do with my lack of trust."

It was all she could manage for now, but she had managed it, and that, Bella realized, was a victory.

Luke worked his jaw, nodding slowly. He looked like someone who had a lot more questions but knew enough not to ask them.

"Why did you say my dad wasn't a good person?"

Bella went cold, as they both turned to see Lily standing in the doorway of the kitchen, a scowl on her face.

"You won't tell me anything about him," Lily continued, her voice going high, "but you'll talk to Luke about him and say nasty things about him. It's not fair!"

She turned and ran.

Bella leaped up from her chair and ran after her daughter, and Luke's inclination to run after them was so strong that he had, in fact, taken a few hurried steps behind them when his mother's voice behind him said, "Luke?" and he finally remembered why he'd come up to the house in the first place.

"Where were you running off to?" his mother asked him. "I wasn't expecting to see you here. Don't you have lessons with that girl?"

"Lily, her name is Lily, Mom," Luke said carefully and clearly. Whether deliberately or as fallout from her own struggles, his mother kept an emotional distance from their guests, preferring to behave almost as if they weren't there. That was a big reason, among many others, that Luke doubted she would ever warm to Bella's idea of turning the house into a bed and breakfast.

Yet, his mother hadn't always been that way. When she was in the role of Sly's wife and partner, the house had often been spilling over with guests, people that his father knew in one way or another.

His mother had been happy then, or at least she had always seemed that way. Maybe it was letting Sly orchestrate things and only having to carry out his wishes that made the difference, but Luke couldn't accept that she had no interest in people at all anymore.

"Would you like some tea?" his mother asked him. He knew that preparing tea was her go-to when there was any threat at all of something becoming unpleasant.

"No thanks, Mom." Luke scratched his head. "But do you have a few minutes to come sit down with me. I think it would be good for us to talk about a few things."

"Oh, Lucas," she said fretfully, "I have so much to do."

Her plaintiveness tore at him, as did her frail shoulders bent over the teapot. But this was the way she had managed to avoid tough conversations since Sly's passing, and although it went against his nature, Luke had to harden himself against giving in again. There was too much at stake.

"This won't take long," he said. "But we do need to talk, Mom."

Carrying her teacup like it weighed about a hundred pounds, his mother walked reluctantly to the table and sat down.

"What is it, Lucas?"

Luke silently prayed for guidance, asking that he be given the words and the right way to convey his questions so that his already skittish mother wouldn't end the conversation before it even started.

"You know I would have been happy to drive you to town if I'd known you needed to go," he began.

"Cal said he was going in, and the time worked, so it was just easier to do it that way," his mother said. "Besides, I figured you would be busy with Bella."

Something about the slight, suggestive emphasis she put on the name made Luke look up and study her face. But his mother kept her eyes on her tea, idly dragging a spoon through it.

Luke decided to push away any questions he might have about her tone and focus on what was really on his mind before his mother decided to retreat and he lost another opportunity.

"What did you and Cal talk about on the drive in?" he asked, trying to sound casual and knowing full well that he wasn't pulling it off.

"The weather," his mother said, giving him a look. "Cal's brother is coming to visit next week," she added. "We talked about that."

Luke drummed his fingers on the table. "Where was your errand? Did Cal go with you or did he just drop you off?"

His mother had been about to take a sip of her tea, but she sat the cup down.

"What is the matter with you, Lucas?" she snapped. "I don't know why you're interrogating me this way."

Luke raked his fingers through his hair and tried to focus on how to ask the questions that he really wanted to ask without sending his mother scurrying like a mouse from a hawk.

It didn't help that a portion of his mind couldn't stop thinking about how Bella was dealing with what Lily overheard or, for that matter, how much he wanted to understand what she had gone through…and maybe be the man who helped her understand that it didn't always have to be that way.

But the fog of retreat and denial was starting to come over his mother's face again, so he blurted out a question before he could second-guess it.

"Do you ever discuss the ranch's finances with Cal?"

His mother looked guilty.

"Cal's pretty tight with the Cooper brothers, isn't he?" Luke mused, thinking out loud, as something curdled in his stomach. "Would he have any reason to tell them that they could get the ranch for a steal?"

His mother's cheeks flamed red, as grief and anger flared into her eyes.

"Your father put us in this position," she cried. "So don't blame me for the people I've had to talk to and the decisions I might have to make."

Luke prepared himself for her to bolt, but instead her shoulders slumped and she sunk into her chair like a marionette whose strings had been cut.

Sly Duffy had been an exacting father, almost impossible to get praise from. He had been loud, always taking over a room, confident to the point of arrogance. Sly had been many things, a great businessman and a protective husband. He'd had both good and bad qualities.

But something Luke knew beyond doubt in the very core of him was that his father would never have intentionally stopped taking care of his family in the best way he knew how or failed to make arrangements to continue that care in the event of his death.

"Mom," he said, folding his hands on the table and leaning forward in earnest. "How many years were you married?"

She blinked at him, so he continued without waiting for her to answer.

"I know it was for a good many years, and, in all that time, did Dad ever treat you disrespectfully or ever do anything to show that he didn't have your best interests at heart?"

His mother shook her head adamantly. "Of course not."

"So there had to be a reason for the investments that he made," Luke rushed on, not willing to relinquish her attention now that he had it. "At the very least, it only makes sense that he had no idea that they were going to turn out to be bad investments. Mom, you must know in your heart that he would never deliberately hurt you or put our home at risk. He must have got some bad advice from someone he trusted. The answer has got to be somewhere."

Something glinted deep in his mother's eyes, just a flicker, but it was there: something that looked like she might finally be willing to dig a little deeper instead of resigning herself to unfortunate circumstances.

"I wouldn't know where to start," she said.

"I can help you," Luke said. "We can go through Dad's files together."

His mother nodded slowly, and it was all he could do not to jump up and fist pump the air.

"Bella sees so much potential here," he said. "We'll get back on our feet again, you'll see."

"You like that woman, don't you?" his mother observed, her eyes now shrewd, though she was careful to keep her tone neutral.

"I do," Luke admitted, not wanting to spoil the progress he'd made. "She's become a good friend."

"Just remember," his mother said, "she's not going to be here much longer. I don't want her tangled up in our family's business any more than she has to be. I haven't decided against selling the ranch yet, and I don't want you thinking that some woman you barely know is going to solve our problems, especially when she's leaving at the end of the summer."

Luke's spirits sank a bit, like a pinhole was slowly letting air out of a tire.

As if I need reminding.

But she wasn't gone yet, and something in him still believed there was time for more than one answered prayer.

Chapter Thirteen

Bella had caught up with Lily as she headed toward the stables and had finally gotten her back to their cabin with the kind of parenting she hated most: a mix of scolding and pleading that Lily see things from her perspective.

Now they were back in the cabin. Lily lay on her back on the bed, staring at her phone, while Bella paced, anxiously wondering what she should say next.

Lily's phone pinged with a message coming in. Bella guessed it was from Alison but decided to try to break the stony silence by asking, "Is that Alison?"

"No," Lily drawled sarcastically. "It's from one of my many other friends."

Bella sent up a quick prayer for patience. She stopped her pacing and went to sit beside Lily on the bed.

Lily squirmed over.

"It's not necessary for you to talk to me like that," she said. "It was a simple question."

Lily sat up and swung her feet over the other side of the bed, turning her back to Bella.

She spoke to the wall, but her words came out clear and sharp. "I don't appreciate you telling some guy that we barely know that my dad wasn't a good person."

Oh, Lord, Bella prayed silently. *What can I say? What can I do?*

No matter how much she thought or prayed about it, it was still far too painful to think about telling Lily the truth. How could she ever share the ugly facts of that night with anyone, let alone her daughter?

Where had God been that night? She'd always had faith, and she still did, but some experiences were enough to make anyone ask why?

"Your father wasn't a good person," Bella said, softly. "I wish I could tell you more, Lily, but can you please trust that the decisions I made are in your best interest."

Lily didn't say anything for a minute then, in a low voice, asked, "But are you going to be okay without Luke after we leave here?"

It was impossible to tell from her tone if it was a simple question or an accusation.

"What…what do you mean?" Bella regretted the jolt of emotion that made her stammer, not exactly conducive to convincing Lily that she didn't know what she was talking about.

Lily stood up and walked around to face her mother.

"Don't think I can't see you and him making goopy eyes at each other. Me and Alison laugh about it."

Bella's face flushed, and she struggled to find an answer, before reminding herself that she didn't have to explain herself to her preteen daughter…especially when she wasn't sure herself what there was to explain.

Part of her was just glad they weren't talking about *him* anymore.

All she knew was that there didn't seem to be any point in staying cooped up in the cabin with a daughter who wasn't happy to be in her company.

"If you want to find Alison and see what she's up to, go ahead," Bella said. She felt like she was shirking her parental duties, but she honestly wasn't sure where to go from here.

"But let me know what you've got planned," she added as Lily smoothed stray hairs into her ponytail and hurried out the door.

Bella didn't want to linger in the cabin alone, with the dissatisfaction of an unfinished conversation swirling through her mind. Yet, it was a conversation that she could never imagine finishing.

She suddenly wanted to scream.

Instead, she opened the door and stepped outside to see Luke walking quickly toward her.

Her heart did a peppy little tap dance at the sight of his smile.

"I made progress," he said.

"That's—great," Bella said, trying to pull herself out of her own fog.

Then Luke's expression changed as he noticed her hesitation.

"How's Lily?" he asked, immediately switching gears. "Did you catch up with her? Please let me know if there's anything I can do."

If Luke Duffy wasn't proof that not all men were selfish and only concerned with their own agendas, Bella didn't know who would be, but her emotional scars still ran deep.

Also, the "goopy-eyed, Alison and I laugh at you" comment wasn't helping.

"Yes, I found her, and she's okay," she answered succinctly, rationalizing to herself that, for all intents and purposes, it was true. Lily had not come to any harm, though it was stretching things a bit—maybe a lot—to say that things were okay between them.

But she didn't need to involve Luke in all of that, despite his expressed willingness.

"I thought you might have crossed paths," Bella added. "She was trying to track Alison down."

"No." Luke shook his head. "I didn't see her, but they must be meeting up at the stables. That was where Alison said she was going."

"So, you were saying you made some progress?" Bella prompted.

"Yes. Would you like to walk with me and hear about it?"

"Of course."

It occurred to Bella again as they walked together how much she loved these surroundings and, particularly, how much she enjoyed observing the way Luke so clearly loved them.

She wasn't quite ready to unravel what that meant for her emotionally, but it strengthened her resolve to help New Hope survive, and it sounded like Luke had some news that would strengthen that possibility.

He led her up to the top of a small hill that overlooked the trees below. At one point, she stumbled a little, and he took her hand to steady her.

She still marveled at how natural it felt for him to touch her and how she was comforted by that touch.

"Can you sit?" Luke eyed Bella's blue jeans, which were still newer and stiffer looking than she would have liked.

The longer she was at the ranch, the more she longed for casual, comfortable clothing, hair that blew freely in the wind, skin that was touched by the sun rather than by a makeup brush.

She knew what she really longed for was an entirely fresh start, not to have to go back and face the challenges of finding new employment and Lily's issues at school. She longed to be someone who wouldn't continually be triggered by things that made her remember that night.

She knew of other women who had survived abuse and assault and had gone on to find themselves in loving, healthy relationships, but because her assault resulted in a pregnancy, she had just never believed the same was possible for her.

But now, with the vast prairie sky above her and Luke Duffy by her side, always taking her needs into account, despite his own challenges, the door of possibilities cracked open and let a ray of light in.

Once again, Luke reached his hand to steady her as Bella lowered herself to sit beside him on the hill.

Then he didn't take his hand away but let it rest on hers as they both gazed out at the scenery that tugged at both their hearts.

She felt so calm and, at the same time, so rejuvenated by the clean air, which was starting to take on the crisp notes of late summer, the scent of the grass, the songs of warblers in the distance, that it took a moment for that to connect.

He hasn't moved his hand.

But instead of the expected urge to yank her hand away as she battled away fear and repulsion, Bella found that his touch became part of the surroundings, soothing yet invigorating.

She turned her head to look at him. He wasn't looking back, still looking out at his family's land. He was close enough that she could see new stubble on his jawline and smell his pine-scented soap and freshly laundered shirt.

If she spoke to him with her head turned in his direction, he would feel her breath on his cheek…

She turned her head back to look outward again.

"Tell me about talking to your mother," she said.

He didn't answer right away then, when he did speak, he said, "I've been thinking about something."

"Oh?" For some reason, Bella's heart sped up a bit but not in an unpleasant way.

Now, he was turning his face to her, his breath warm and smelling of minty toothpaste.

"I was thinking about how we both have stuff going on," he said, "and how we've kind of danced around it. I mean you know something about my situation, but I really don't know anything about yours, not really. So, I was just thinking." Now a note of longing came into his voice. "How good it would be for both of us if, instead of avoiding the hard things, we both had someone we could really trust to open up to." His voice lowered until it was almost a whisper. "I don't know about you, Bella, but I want someone in my life that I can share it all with."

Tension, that was not fear, pulsed in the air between them. *What did he mean by "all"?*

There was still a part of her, a part still larger than anything else, that knew she would never completely open up about what had happened to her, a part that knew, sadly, that because she was never going to be willing to do that she would never fully enjoy what Luke seemed to be implying.

And yet…

Another part of her, a small but strongly hopeful part of her, knew that if she turned her face to meet his, their lips would be just a breath away, and it would only take a kiss to close the space between them.

Bella turned her head; she saw both question and answer in his eyes.

And she closed the gap.

Her lips were soft, warm and sweet. Her hair and skin smelled both of herself and of the land around them. The kiss was utterly…right. It was safe to say that he had never before experienced such a sensation of adventure and of coming home at the same time.

Luke only had seconds to process all of those sensations before Bella pulled back and blinked at him as if coming out of a long dream.

"I didn't know that was going to happen," she said, slightly breathless.

"I'm glad it did."

Her cheeks flushed prettily, and then, although she had stopped kissing him—and he couldn't quite tell how she felt about it, even though she had been the instigator—she remained sitting close to him, her shoulder pressed against his, sending waves of warmth through him.

They shared silence together, but just as Luke was thinking that he could stay by this woman's side, surrounded by the land that he loved, for a very long time, Bella shifted away from him and said, "I like you, Luke, more than I thought possible. But the summer is almost over, and I think we both need to focus on the things we need to do."

"I know that," Luke said on a sigh. "I just want us to be a team and enjoy all the time we can together. Is it at all possible we can do that?"

Bella was silent until it was on the edge of being uncomfortable, but she finally answered, "Yes, I think we can do that. So…tell me about talking to your mom."

"I will," Luke said, "but I do have one more question for you first, something I've been wanting to ask you since you arrived."

She shifted and he could tell that curiosity and concern were mingling.

"Okaaay?" she said.

"So… *Arabella*?" Luke asked, grinning. "What's that about?"

A snorting laugh exploded out of Bella's mouth. She quickly covered her mouth with her hands and giggled until her eyes watered.

"Ahh," she said, gasping and wiping tears away with the back of her hands. "I was definitely not expecting that."

"I think you mentioned an aunt?" Luke guessed teasingly, his heart floating away on the sound of Bella's laughter.

"A great-aunt," she confirmed. "Not rich, or at least if she was, she never let us know. Believe it or not, my mother just liked the name. She said it sounded like it belonged in a storybook."

"I wish I could have spent more of the summer getting to know more about you and your family," Luke mused.

Bella was silent, and he felt her subtly shift away.

His heart stopped its floating. Sweet kisses or not, it seemed that there would always be this wall between them.

"So, about my mom," he said briskly and relayed their conversation to her.

"That's good," Bella said, nodding when he was done. "That's progress for sure."

"I know I have to be more patient with her," Luke said. "She's been through a lot and there are so many things going on that she doesn't understand. I can't think of anything worse than thinking your spouse has done something untrustworthy with no way to confront the issue."

"Yes, she's doing the best she can," Bella said. "So are you."

The week continued on. Luke noticed that Bella was finding every opportunity she could to talk to his mother, and he could tell that she was slowly getting through to her about the possibilities still inherent at New Hope.

Meanwhile, he continued his sessions with Lily, and Alison had become a regular part of the lessons too. He knew next to nothing about preteen girls and their relationships with their mothers, but even he could tell that some of the ease and trust they had between them was missing, and it was because of what Bella couldn't share with Lily about her father.

What happened to her, Lord? Who hurt her?

But it was none of his business, and he found that, as long as he didn't edge too close to that or any other topic that caused Bella to withdraw into herself, becoming aloof and business-like again, she was warm and wonderful company.

Somewhere in him, Luke knew it couldn't continue like this. It wouldn't be enough. He wanted a true emotional bond. But he tried to reason with himself that it was better than nothing, and he tried not to think of how rapidly the end of summer was approaching.

At supper on Saturday night, Bella said, "I don't want to have left this place without going to a Sunday morning service at the chapel. Who's with me?"

"You can count me in," Luke said readily, although Bella's eyes were on Lily when she asked the question.

"I had just planned to watch a sermon broadcast online," his mother said. "I want to get to Sly's papers as soon as I can today."

"I'm going to help you with that, Mom," Luke reminded her. But he wasn't as worried as he had been. His mother finally was no longer seeming so vague and unfocused, and he was finally able to remember that she had been a strong, intelligent partner to his father, a partner who had been stunned not only by his death but also by the financial decisions he had made.

"What about you, Lily?" Bella asked.

Luke could tell how hard she was trying not to seem like she wanted it too much, and he hoped Lily would say yes.

But Lily and Alison exchanged glances, their noses scrunched.

"Could we just hang out here?" Alison asked.

"I guess I don't have a problem with that," Luke said slowly. "But I can't answer for Lily."

He didn't believe in forcing anyone to go to church and

knew he hadn't been setting the best example himself lately. He still started his days by spending time in the Word, and he prayed throughout the day. But interacting with others there while he had so much on his mind just didn't appeal to him.

The chapel did seem, though, like the perfect middle ground, and the thought of sitting there with Bella by his side was a pleasing one.

"You don't have to go if you don't want to," Bella said.

Luke could hear the effort it was taking for her not to sound disappointed. He wondered if church was something they were used to doing together and if this rebellion on Lily's part was something new and connected to the emotional distance that had sprung up between them because of the matter of Lily's father.

I wish Bella would talk to someone.

Lily showed little concern about her mother's feelings— being a typical preteen, Luke supposed—as she and Alison exchanged grins and began to shovel their food more quickly into their mouths.

"I want you to stay close by," Luke cautioned, "and let your grandma know whatever you're doing."

"We will," Alison said, and both girls nodded.

After supper, Luke left another phone message for Brett. He prayed that his resentful feelings toward his brother and his wife would subside.

The sky as Sunday morning dawned was alive with the best of the Creator's paint palette, giving its silent praise to His glory.

Luke knotted his tie and studied his freshly shaven face in the mirror. His eyes asked what the day would bring.

Bella and Lily had remained in their cabin for breakfast. His mother said that Bella had come in earlier to pick up some coffee and juice, along with some fruit and yogurt, to take back.

"Did she say why?" Luke was unaccountably nervous that

she might have changed her mind about joining him, and he realized how very much he wanted to attend church with her.

"No, she didn't say anything."

So when he stepped outside and saw Bella coming out wearing a beautiful white sundress, adorned with a pattern of violets, with a lightweight purple cardigan over her shoulders, he let his breath out in a rush of grateful relief.

"You look lovely," he said.

She attempted to shrug off the compliment, but he saw her mouth curve in a shyly pleased smile.

"You're wearing a tie," she commented. "I wasn't sure how people would dress."

"Some might be casual," Luke said, "but wearing a tie to church has been drilled into me since I was a kid, so…"

"I hope this is okay." Bella smoothed her dress.

"It's perfect."

You're perfect.

She smiled. "I'm glad you think so."

There weren't many people there when they arrived at the chapel, but Pastor Stewart greeted them all with a smile, showing gratitude for who was there.

"Where would you like to sit?" Luke asked, and Bella pointed to a spot near the front.

It felt so good, so *right*, Luke thought with her sitting by his side, listening attentively. With Gwen, he'd always suspected that being seen in church was more important to her than what she could actually learn there.

At one point, Bella leaned closer, treating him to a whiff of a fresh, citrusy scent, and murmured, "I wish I'd brought a notebook and pen."

Then the pastor was saying something from the pulpit that caused her to go very still and silent.

"You know that saying, you're only as sick as the secrets you keep?" he said, pacing a bit and gesturing. "Well, in the book of Luke, the Bible says that what we hide will be shown and what we keep secret will be made known. Now, I don't believe in any way that God is saying this so that we feel threatened or ashamed. I believe that He's letting us know that we don't have to keep the secrets that are making us sick and that when we share them, He will still be there to accept us and to love us."

After the service, Luke and Bella both shook Pastor Stewart's hand and thanked him for the service, but Luke caught something subdued and troubled in her voice.

"Some folks like to stay around for coffee and cookies after," Pastor Stewart suggested. "I'm afraid the cookies aren't homemade, but it should be a friendly group."

Luke looked at Bella, trying to gauge her reaction.

"That sounds really nice," she said, "but maybe next time. I want to get back and see how my daughter is doing."

She smiled as she said it, but Luke wondered if the sermon had exposed a nerve and she wasn't about to give anyone a chance to poke at it.

Does that include me?

Back in the car, he did up his seat belt, but instead of starting the car, he drummed his fingers lightly on the steering wheel.

"Is everything okay?" Bella asked uneasily.

He turned to her. "I know someone has hurt you," he said. "And I could tell that what the pastor had to say today hit hard. Bella…do you think it's time to stop keeping the secret that's making you sick?"

Chapter Fourteen

Bella's first impulse was to tell Luke that he had no idea what he was talking about.

But something—*Is that You, Lord?*—stopped her and made her think twice about her habitual reaction.

Because Luke was absolutely right: the sermon today had hit her hard.

She was so used to keeping the secret of that night, so used to pretending that she was fine, or even that it had all been some kind of nightmare, that she didn't allow herself to stop and consider all of the ways it had an impact on her. She hid behind her business successes, her carefully curated style, a veneer of perfection that kept danger at a distance.

But now she realized that all this time she'd been keeping good things at a distance too. She'd never allowed herself the possibility of a real, loving relationship, and now her refusal to be honest was threatening to rip apart her relationship with her daughter.

She swallowed and her dry throat ached a little. "Could we maybe go for a drive somewhere?"

"Whatever you like," Luke said. "But I thought you wanted to see how Lily was doing."

"I do... I..." Her thoughts spun. "I'll send her a text. I'm sure she doesn't mind having a bit more of a break from me."

Luke reached out and squeezed her hand.

Bella sent off the message and watched the screen for a reply, which came in quickly.

"The girls are fine," she told Luke.

He nodded and checked his watch before starting the car.

"The chapel lets out a little earlier than the churches in town," he said. "If we head to Jacob's now, we could beat the after-church rush."

"Sure, that sounds good."

"We can talk on the way," Luke said. "I mean," he added hurriedly, "if you want to."

For a little while, they did drive without talking, a Christian music station playing softly in the background.

Bella contemplated how even sitting in a car alone with a man was a step she hadn't known she was capable of until this summer. She snuck a peek at Luke from under her eyelids. She liked the way he kept his eyes steady on the road but still managed to give off a vibe that he was aware of her presence and would be willing to listen if she was willing to share.

She allowed herself to really consider how it would feel not to carry the burden alone.

Can I do this, Lord?

Maybe she could…with His help.

"Lily's father…" she began and stopped. Even saying those two words caused her throat to clog up, her heart to start pounding.

Luke eased the car over. He didn't touch her; he didn't say a word, but somehow everything about him radiated *I'm here*.

Finally ready to move on, Bella shared the story of that fateful night. As she shared the full story for the first time, she felt a sense of release as the hurt, anger and fear were lifted off of her shoulders.

She couldn't say any more, but it was more than she had ever said and it was enough.

She wanted to sob, no longer with hidden pain but with the relief of sharing her burdensome secret at last.

Luke's eyes were stormy, not with contempt or disgust for her but with such sorrow and compassion that the tears of grief and rage that Bella had held back for so long finally poured out of her.

She sobbed harshly and didn't try to stop herself.

Finally, after what simultaneously seemed like too short a time and her entire lifetime, Bella drew a couple of shaky breaths.

"I—I think that's definitely what people call an ugly cry," she said with grim humor.

"May I?" Luke asked very softly.

She understood that he was asking if he could offer her physical touch for comfort. She also knew that he would always respect her boundaries, even if she chose to never let him touch her again.

It was knowing this that led Bella to lean into his arms and kiss the side of his stubbly cheek, inhaling his comforting smell.

Snuggled into him, she quietly told him the repercussions of that night, most significantly finding out that she was pregnant. She told him of how painfully ashamed she had been to allow her parents to think that the night in question was simply a mistake because she couldn't bear to hurt them with the truth of it.

"Thankfully, they couldn't help loving Lily," she said. "They're very good to her."

"And you've never told Lily anything about her father?" Luke asked.

Bella pulled back and looked at him.

"How can I?" she asked with a deep sadness. "I don't want her to know what happened to me, but most of all I don't want her to think for a single second that she's unwanted. It's a paradox. I'd do anything if I could go back in time and make sure that night never happened. But I wouldn't give up Lily for anything in the world."

Luke nodded. "I get that."

Bella leaned back against him. They were quiet for a moment. She could feel his chest lifting her gently as he breathed in and out.

He ran a gentle hand down her hair. "You know none of it was your fault, don't you?" he asked.

"My heart knows it," Bella said after a pause. "But my head keeps telling me all the things I could have done differently that night."

"It wasn't your fault," Luke repeated. "None of it." He hesitated, drawing in a deep breath. "Would you ever think about telling Lily? Or at least telling her enough so that she understands where you're coming from and maybe it wouldn't be driving such a wedge between you?"

Once again, Bella pulled back and studied his face.

"I don't think so." She cared a great deal for Luke, more than she believed it was possible to care for any man, but she was more than a little frustrated that he didn't get what a bad choice that would be.

He rubbed the frown line between her brows with his forefinger like it could make it vanish.

"What if I was with you?"

"I think that would make it worse," Bella sighed. "She already thinks I'm disloyal to her dad, who she imagines to be this great guy that I'm just keeping from her for some reason, and that there's something between us."

Something between us. The words hung like a suspension bridge between them.

"There could be something between us," Luke said, between a breath and a whisper, so softly that if she hadn't been so close, she wouldn't have heard him at all.

Her heart wanted it badly, but her head made Bella protest. "I don't see how. We both have so much to figure out. I need to find a job. I was hoping everything would fall into place and work out for both of us, but time is running out, and I don't see that happening."

She expected Luke to agree, but instead she felt his warm lips at the crown of her head, and he said, "But what if there was time? What if we could make the time?"

She shook her head. "That's not possible. Lily has to get back to school, and like I said, I need to find work."

"There's the school in town here," Luke persisted, "and I think that Alison will still be here and be starting there herself soon. There are jobs, maybe not what you're used to doing, but there must be something you can do."

Why was he being so stubborn about this? Why was he giving her hope like it was the most reasonable thing in the world to do so?

Bella realized that, although she believed in God, it had been a long, long time since she'd trusted Him with the details.

Lord, is this Your way of reminding me that I can...that I should?

But she had to ask, "What if your mother still wants to sell the ranch?"

Luke took his time answering. That was one of the things she loved best about him, that he didn't blurt things off the top of his head but took time to consider how he really felt about something.

Loved about him...

"I've decided to leave it in God's hands," he said, unknowingly reflecting her own thoughts, which caused a flutter within Bella at the way they connected.

"I've finally convinced my mother that all may not be as it seems to be," he continued, "so I hope that means that she's willing to dig into things a little deeper. I think the ranch belongs in our family, but if God has a different idea, I need to trust Him with that. Listen, Arabella…" He used her full name with the fondest smile Bella had ever seen. "The important thing to me now is that we know we are here for each other. There's still a lot to figure out—I'm not denying that. But why stay in our own corners, battling against the world like we have to do it all on our own when we can be there for each other. Please…let me be there for you. Are you willing to do that?"

Something that she had kept long buried—so deeply buried that she almost forgot that she had it—swelled up within Bella.

It was the willingness to trust and count on another human being. Even as she said the simple word, she could not believe how much hope could be packed into a single syllable.

"Yes."

Luke savored a happiness that he had almost stopped believing was possible.

Yes, he wanted to save New Hope, yes it was still important to him to honor his father's legacy. He loved the home and the land around it in the intrinsic, unthinking way that someone loved taking their next breath.

But now, instead of feeling like it was a losing battle that he fought on a lonely hill, he had a mutual support system going with the most beautiful, complex woman he had ever known.

Hearing what she had gone through only made him admire and respect her more.

His phone chimed, and when he looked at the message, a frown brought his eyebrows together.

"What's wrong?" Bella asked.

"It's my mother," he said. "She wants me to get home right away…"

He scratched his lower lip and read the message again.

"She's fired Cal Wayman."

A little while later, his mother sat at the kitchen table with Luke and Bella. Bella had offered to leave, to give them privacy, but she assured her that it was okay for her to stay.

Lily and Alison were out at the stables visiting the horses.

His mother had several ledgers and documents spread out across the table, along with printouts of correspondence between Sly and Cal.

It appeared that once Nora Duffy had a fire lit under her, she remembered all the ways that her late husband had respected her and how she had been a strong partner for him.

She'd also remembered the man who wouldn't have put his family or their home at risk in any way if he'd known that was what he was doing.

Luke and Bella took some time to go over the things that Nora had come across, and it was clear that Cal Wayman, probably by using the influence of his years of service and close working relationship with Sly, had convinced Sly to make some investments that were designed to benefit Cal, not the Duffy family or their ranch.

Luke sat back. His neck and shoulders ached from hunching over the papers, but the unease that went through him was worse.

"You say you fired Cal, Mom?"

She lifted her chin. "I most certainly did. I should report him to the authorities for the way he's taking advantage of all of us."

"He's never scheduled to work on a Sunday," Luke said. "How did—how did the firing come about?"

He could see by Bella's troubled eyes that she knew what he was concerned about.

"I called him," his mother said, now defensive, "and I told him that I don't want him setting foot in this house or on this land ever again. It's the truth, I don't."

A dull ache began to thud behind Luke's eyes, and anxiety was clearly written across Bella's usually unflappable face.

Partners, he thought.

But why wasn't that helping him to feel better?

"Did you tell him why?" He feared he already knew the answer.

"Of course I did," his mother exploded, flapping her arms a little. It would have made a comical sight, except the situation was so *not* comical.

"You can't do that, Mom," Luke said, speaking slowly and clearly in an effort not to betray his own knotted stomach. "You can't just call someone up who's worked for us as long as Cal Wayman has and hurl accusations at him, no matter how true we think or know they are, and fire him."

His chest clenched with a sure knowledge. "He's going to come for us hard."

He took a few deep breaths and returned his attention to the papers before him, mumbling, "We'll have to pull this together in a way that shows anyone looking into it a clear picture of what happened."

Alison and Lily came into the kitchen.

Luke suddenly recalled something that Sly used to say: that sometimes life would knock you down, and then it would kick you.

He immediately knew by the look on Alison's face that the kick was coming.

The papers around him blurred into the background as he asked, "Alison, what's wrong?"

"Mom and Dad…they're…"

Lily patted her shoulder, her face drenched in sympathy.

"Dad just texted me. They're getting a divorce."

Somewhere in his spinning head, something focused into a sharp, angry thought.

Only Brett and Gwen would make some big dramatic show of trying to infuse new life into their marriage, would neglect their daughter while doing so, and would inform her that hey, this didn't work the way we'd hoped, by a text message.

At a loss for words, he got up and went to his niece. He wasn't sure if he should hug her or not, but she nestled close to him and sniffed loudly.

"I'm so sorry," Bella said. "I know there probably isn't anything I can do, but if there is…"

Bella.

Luke had almost forgotten she was there.

He was stunned that he could have done so, so soon after they had promised that they wouldn't let each other struggle through things alone. But really, she was right. What could she do?

It had been a lovely thought, and on some level, Luke had truly meant everything he said, but what had he been thinking?

A beautiful, strong-minded woman and her horse-whisperer daughter had arrived at the ranch at the beginning of summer, and he had let himself get swept away. He had allowed himself to believe that there was something he could put his mind and heart into other than doing his bedraggled best to save his family and their home.

But now they had a disgruntled former employee on their hands, his brother's marriage was falling apart and he was left to pick up the pieces of his niece's shattered heart, and he still had no idea how he was going to bring New Hope back to its former glory days.

Sometimes, boy, the best thing you can do for yourself is recognize your own limitations.

The memory of his father's voice sounded so loudly in his head that Luke almost cringed.

Well, his dad might have been proud that he certainly knew his limitations: he wasn't going to be able to be who he needed to be for his family and start up a new relationship at the same time.

As much as he wanted to.

He turned to Bella, praying that his heart didn't show in his eyes. He didn't want to make this any harder than it already was.

Alison had let go of his arm and had tugged Lily to the side, saying something to her in a low voice that Luke couldn't quite make out.

"Thank you for the offer," Luke addressed to Bella. He could hear the stiff formality in his voice. "You know, I hate to do this to you, but with only a few days left in your stay here, feel free to use the accommodations and visit or ride the horses as you like. I really don't think I can teach Lily any more than I have—she's a natural, and I hope her time here has helped you both. But, as you've heard, there are some unexpected family issues that I have to focus on. I would be happy to refund a portion of your money."

At that suggestion, Bella's eyes flared with hurt and anger mingled with a thousand questions.

But she didn't ask any of them. Instead, she said, "Lily, let's go back to our cabin and let the Duffys talk."

The Duffys.

She had adopted his formality, and he could only imagine what she must be thinking.

"But, Mom…" Lily began to protest.

"Now, Lily," Bella said in a tone that did not allow for any arguments. It was like a door being slammed shut.

When her eyes met his as they departed, Luke felt in the core of him that the slammed door was meant for him too.

But there was nothing he could do about that now. He might well love her, and maybe someday, if things ever got straightened out with his family and his home, he would be able to tell her that.

Maybe…but he wasn't counting on it.

He turned to his mother. "I'll call Cal back," he said, not relishing the thought whatsoever. "At the very least, we have to give him notice, offer him some kind of severance."

"Why should we have to do that?" Nora protested. "He cheated us already and ruined what was ours. None of it makes sense."

No, it did not. Luke had to agree with that sentiment as he ran a hand down his face, closing his eyes against the headache that wanted to pound its way in.

It was difficult to make sense of it all. If Cal wanted to scoop the ranch from them at a low price and take it over, why were the Cooper brothers involved?

He wasn't going to give up on getting answers to those questions, but in the meantime, he had to conduct himself in the way he knew was best.

"We're doing it because it's good business and because it's the right thing to do," he said. "We're not going to lower our standards because of someone else's behavior. We'll have to trust that somewhere down the line it's going to catch up with him."

For once in his life, Luke was one hundred percent sure that Sly Duffy would have approved of his decision.

It was too bad that making his father's memory proud no longer felt like enough.

Chapter Fifteen

In their cabin, Lily took up her all too familiar sulking-on-her-bed pose.

In a distant part of her, Bella understood that the matter between them regarding the identity of Lily's father was still present and probably only enhanced by recent happenings. But somehow, she couldn't muster up the energy to deal with the worry of that on top of the other things she was struggling with: other things that pressed more tightly and immediately on her heart than something that had happened in the past.

Why can't he love me back?

She had been sure, so sure, that it was love that everything between her and Luke had been leading to.

She hadn't known she even wanted that, and now it seemed as if she was going to have to let it go.

She shouldn't have told him about that night. The certainty of that slammed into her like a freight train. He might have been starting to care for her, but that was an ugly experience to dump on anyone. It would have been better if she had kept that to herself.

Well, she'd learned her lesson, and she wouldn't be doing that again, not that she expected to have the chance to.

A strong urge to get away from Luke and the ranch and all the wonderful, new and confusing emotions bubbled up in Bella, and it took all her self-control not to throw her and

Lily's clothes into their suitcases and drag her daughter out to the car to head home as quickly as they could.

Home… For a moment, she didn't even know what that word meant anymore, or what was waiting for her there. When she tried to bring their small house to mind, all she could see were rolling hills and trees, prairie skies, a house that still held so much potential…and a stormy-eyed rancher who loved it all.

And she realized that, despite his dismissing her, she still wanted to help. Not only because she cared deeply for Luke but also because she refused to let herself down.

He may not love her, but Bella had never been one to give up on a task she'd set her mind to, and she wasn't going to start now.

"I want to make a drive into town," she said to Lily. "You're welcome to come, or you can spend time with Alison, if it's okay with Nora and Luke."

She knew what option her daughter would choose if it was available to her. She couldn't help hoping it would be. She needed the drive to clear her head, and she hoped that Jacob would be free for a chat when she landed in on his café.

She'd only met the man once, but after silently praying, she was assured in her heart that it was the right choice.

"I thought I had to stay here." Lily eyed her suspiciously.

"No—I just wanted to make sure that we gave them their privacy."

If they were still in the midst of things, Lily would need to come with her. Either way, she was going.

Lily sent a message off on her phone. A few seconds later, she said, "Okay, I'm going up. Al says that her grandma and Luke are in her grandpa's old office talking about something, and she's pretty bored."

"Make sure it's okay with them too," Bella prompted and was rewarded with an eye roll.

But Lily sent another message and, after a minute or two, nodded.

"Okay, I won't be long," Bella said.

A short time later, she was driving toward town.

A hint of autumn permeated the air. There were still more green leaves than red or brown, but the end of August had always signaled to Bella that a change was coming.

A change and still so many unanswered questions.

Would the answer to any of them lead to a new start for her and Lily, even if it wasn't with Luke?

The True to You café wasn't completely empty, Bella hadn't expected a popular place like it would be, but most of the customers seemed to be sitting out of earshot, and she hoped to claim one of the stools at the counter and talk to Jacob while he prepared food and beverages.

She recognized a woman sitting in a booth, sipping coffee and studying a newspaper with an anxious expression. It was Aubrey, the horse trainer they'd met the first time Luke had brought her and Lily to the café.

Bella promised herself she would say hello when she was done talking to Jacob.

Once again, she breathed a prayer for guidance before heading to the counter and making herself comfortable on one of the stools.

Jacob finished pouring coffee into two mugs that were painted to look like wise old owls before turning. His eyes widened when he saw her, then his welcoming smile crinkled them at the corners.

"Bella," he said. "Great to see you."

He radiated hospitality and comfort, a human safe harbor. If he wondered why she was alone, he didn't ask. But she somehow trusted that he understood she was there for a reason and that he would be patient until she was ready to share what that was.

It struck Bella that Jacob made two now: two men she completely trusted.

Surely, God had brought her to Trydale for a reason. Was she finally ready for her heart to be healed?

"Something I can get you?" Jacob offered, performing his proprietor's duties while a warm concern lingered in his dark eyes.

"Coffee would be great, thanks. Black, please."

He poured it into a mug decorated with moose antlers and handed it to her, then turned and passed a plate of pancakes and sausage to a server who stood nearby.

The smell was tantalizing, but Bella knew she'd better get talking before the pace picked up, which could happen at any moment.

"I need to talk to you about something," Bella began. "I hope you don't think it's too strange me coming to you this way, because we just met. But I know you know Luke Duffy and his family well."

Jacob had been wiping the counter using large circular motions. The cloth didn't stop moving, but the incline of his head told Bella he was listening.

It all poured out of her: the struggles Lily had been having in school with her anxiety, which led to them coming to New Hope; Lily's way with the horses and unexpected friendship with Alison; her own bond and connection with Luke; her quitting her job, basically because it was that or be fired; what they knew so far about shady dealings at the ranch and her yearning to do something about it that would both fix the Duffys' issues and start her on a new path.

Bella took a deep inhale of air that tasted like freedom.

But then reality hit again, pulling her breath out of her in a big whoosh.

"But I can't stay," she said, trying to shrug away a sadness that ran bone deep. "I need to find work, and there's really nothing for me to do here, as much as I want there to be, and my daughter has to get back to school."

And I think Luke Duffy might have shut me out for good after what I shared with him.

Jacob remained quiet. He took a glass out of the dishwasher, inspected it and wiped off a spot with a cloth.

With his eyes still on the glass, he said, "The thing we all seem to forget sometimes is that we don't have to keep doing what we've always done."

"What do you mean?"

His dark eyes shifted to hers. "I mean that there would be plenty for you to do here if you really wanted to stay. It might not be what you've always done or what you're used to doing, but you'd find work if you needed to."

Bella nodded slowly, taking in his words but still not fully processing them.

Jacob went back to the dishwasher. "The whole town knows what the ranch has been going through," he said, "and we'd all love to help, but we can't until the Duffys realize that they don't have to keep doing things the same old way."

Bella wanted to ask what he meant again, but after a pause, he kept talking as if he'd anticipated her question.

"Don't get me wrong," Jacob said. "Sly Duffy was a great man, a true family man, a business man and an asset to this town. But I think one of the greatest legacies he left his family was that of pride. He wanted things done a certain way. It was important to him to keep up a certain image, and he didn't like to go back on any decisions he made, even when it would have been best to do so, and I'm sure that his family has kept doing things his way out of loyalty to his memory."

"Like keeping the same staff on," Bella mused, half to herself.

She wondered how much Jacob really knew, as opposed to going by his instincts, which she suspected were formidable. She didn't feel it was her place, though, to say what Luke and Nora had discovered about the late patriarch's financial decisions.

Instead, she asked cautiously, "Do you think Cal Wayman wants to own the ranch?"

Aubrey put her paper down. Her brown eyes snapped.

"Excuse me for butting in," she said. "I haven't been here long, but even I've heard the talk. Some brothers that I don't think anyone thinks much of want to buy it for the land. As far as I can tell, they want to bulldoze everything and build a hotel and casino there. I imagine they're going to cut Cal Wayman in for his part in driving down the price. At least, I'm assuming that was his intent when he put the family in a position of being unable to save the ranch."

A pure, cold anger coursed through Bella on behalf of Luke and his family.

"Has anyone thought to tell them this?" she demanded.

"I don't even really know them," Aubrey said, raising her hands in a "don't shoot the messenger" gesture. "I just know what I've heard."

"I'm sorry, I didn't mean to snap," Bella said.

"That's okay," Aubrey said, nodding. "I get that there's something between you and the son. I could see it the first time I met you. It's natural you'd be protective of his interests."

Bella opened her mouth to protest, fearing that she resembled a gaped-mouth fish.

Aubrey picked up her coffee mug and drained it, then folded

up her newspaper, not appearing to notice the emotional up-heaval she'd caused.

"If you want to put a word in his ear," Aubrey said as she put her payment and a tip on the counter. "Please tell him that I hope they're able to save the ranch. I'd make a great horse trainer for them, and my rates are good."

"I will," Bella said automatically.

"There's nothing between Luke Duffy and I." She finally got the words out after Aubrey was out the door.

Jacob was watching his café fill up, putting on a fresh pot of coffee, stirring a pot of something that smelled fresh and earthy. Yet, Bella knew he'd heard everything that Aubrey had said to her and also her too late protest. Despite his flurry of activity, she was sure he was holding back a smile.

She waited for a lull. She wasn't ready to leave the cozy atmosphere or its kind and wise proprietor. She could picture Luke coming here as a small boy, seeking comfort and reas-surance.

She felt a tug of affection for that little boy…who had grown up to be a man she realized she could care deeply about… whom she did care deeply about.

Was Aubrey right?

Jacob delivered platters of pancakes and eggs and bacon. In between the contented munching of the first morning rush and the onset of the second one, he offered Bella a refill and a menu.

"You heard what Aubrey said?" Bella asked, knowing she didn't have to explain which comments she referred to.

Jacob nodded, a warm twinkle in his eye.

"What do you think?"

"I think that I can't say for other people if there's something between them or not. But," he added off of the look she gave him, "I would say that how much you want to help him and how much you want to stay says something, wouldn't you?"

He turned and stirred the simmering pot again. "Now, it's up to you to decide what that is."

Bella's phone chimed, forestalling her next remark.

She read the message, and a blast of icy fear immediately went through her.

It was from Luke, and it said Come right away. We don't know where the girls are.

Luke paced the kitchen floor, alternately calling and messaging Alison's phone, but the calls went straight to voicemail and his texts remained unanswered. He had looked in the most obvious places and tried numerous times to reach his niece before alerting Bella to the issue.

Bella, who'd done her own disappearing act.

They weren't young children, he reminded himself. They knew enough not to wander into the creek, and Alison knew the lay of the land. She wasn't going to get lost.

But still his thudding heart protested that they weren't in a good emotional space, not with Alison having just received the news about her parents' separation and the tension between Lily and her mother over her father's identity.

Who knew what kind of rash decisions they might make?

Dear Lord, please protect them. Please help all of us through these difficult times.

He absolutely knew that he was including Bella and Lily in that prayer. No matter what the circumstances were, setting aside that he didn't think there was any way that she planned to stay, he could no longer completely separate his life and his emotions from the fact that he had met this strong woman and would never forget her...for all the good that did him.

Beneath his concern for Alison and Lily's whereabouts

lingered an unsettled clenching in his stomach that told him that he had automatically pushed Bella away as soon as family pressure was on again. He hadn't meant to do that; it was a reflexive reaction.

But what must she be thinking about him creating distance between them so soon after she'd revealed her assault to him? Would she think he judged her?

He didn't judge her, he respected and admired her, except his actions said otherwise.

And now he'd sent her a panicky message that involved her daughter, probably putting her into an anxiety-fueled tailspin.

He heard a car pull up, and he ran to the door and flung it open to see Bella exiting her car and hurrying toward the house.

She didn't look like she was in a tailspin. She looked anxious, yes, but also strong and determined.

She also looked wet. Luke realized that rain was pelting down; the sky had darkened ominously, and thunder rumbled in the not too far distance.

He had been so wrapped up in his concerns and regrets that he hadn't even noticed the signs that a storm was coming.

He grabbed one of his jackets from a hook by the door and ran to meet Bella, draping it over her head and putting one arm around her waist to guide her inside.

"I'll find the girls," he promised her. "You can wait with my mother. I'm so sorry this happened. But I promise I'll find them."

"Luke, wait."

Her clear, unwavering tone stopped him. He realized that her hands gripped his arms. Water dripped from her hair and clothes and made a small pool at their feet.

But her eyes were watching his.

"*We* will find the girls," she said. "We're going to pray together, and we will find them."

Luke studied her eyes and saw something there. Something that showed not only trust that Lily and Alison would be found or come home safely but also something deeper... something that said that she trusted that they could accomplish anything together.

"How can you be so sure?" he asked, not just about this moment but about all of it.

She slid her hands down his arms and grasped his hands instead.

"I had a good talk with Jacob at the café," she said. "I have so much to tell you once the girls are back. He said some things and asked me some questions that made me realize many things."

"Jacob has a way of doing that," Luke said softly. His heart pounded while his mind raced with all of the questions he wanted to ask.

But she bowed her head and waited, counting on him to lead the way in prayer.

Something like galloping horses stamped down the fence that Luke had erected in his heart.

It seemed like his whole life he was waiting for assurance from his father that he trusted him to handle things, and since his father had passed, he'd needed that vote of confidence from his mother.

But here now was this woman, this woman who had survived and had raised a smart, sensitive daughter on her own, placing her hands in his—even after her daughter had gone missing on his watch—without showing any doubt that he would handle the situation.

That they would handle it together.

The galloping silenced, and a still, soft voice spoke to his heart.

You could always handle things. You just had to believe it yourself.

Maybe, Luke thought, *with God's help I will finally be able to believe that is true.*

He gave Bella's hands a little squeeze and began to pray.

But as soon as a few words were out of his mouth, the front door burst open and Lily and Alison tumbled in, drenched and shouting apologies.

Lily went straight to her mother and hugged her. Bella hugged her back.

"Thank God," she kept saying. "Thank You, God."

Luke stepped forward and opened his arms to Alison. She hesitated only briefly then stepped into them. He was immediately wet and chilly. It was wonderful.

Nora had heard the clamor and came out to join them. Luke begged her with his eyes not to say anything.

"Mom, I'm so sorry," Luke heard Lily say to her mother. "Al and I were talking, and she reminded me how blessedI am to have a mom like you and that I should be grateful for what I have. I won't bug you about things anymore."

'You're not bugging me, Lily-pad," Bella said with a catch in her voice. "There are…there are just some things I don't know how to tell you, or know if you're ready to hear, but we'll figure it out, I promise."

"I'm sorry too," Alison said, easing herself out of Luke's hug but still staying close. "Hearing about Mom and Dad, I just had to get away, and I dragged Lily with me."

"We'll talk about all of that later," Luke said. "You girls should run up and dry off and get into some warm clothes."

"You can borrow something of mine," Alison told Lily as they climbed the stairs.

"You're not alone in this, Alison," Luke called after her. "We're here and we love you."

When the girls were gone, he turned and saw Bella watching him. Her expression was soft but intent.

"You're not alone in this either," she said, stepping toward him. "You're not alone in any of it, and I'm not either. The whole town wants to help the ranch if you'd let them, and Jacob reminded me that if I really want to start over, I can find a way to do it."

Luke couldn't find the words to ask the questions that he wanted to ask. He wanted Bella to stay, more than anything in the world he wanted that. But he didn't want her to stay because she was hiding from her past or to regret leaving her life behind.

His eyes must have spoken the question for him, because Bella leaned forward and planted a soft kiss on his mouth.

"I'm not running away," she said, still standing so close that he could feel her sweet breath on his face. "I want to be here, Luke. I want to be with you. I've realized that… I love you."

Oh God, could it be possible?

He saw the answer in her eyes. Yes, it was not only possible, it was true.

"I love you too," he said, returning the kiss. "I feel like I've known you all my life. I know you're the one that God has chosen for me." He hesitated, trying to push back the intrusion of other thoughts on the happiest moment of his life.

"What is it?" Bella asked, gazing at him with her heart in her clear blue eyes.

"It's just that there's still the ranch. I don't know what's going to happen with Alison. Lily has to go to school…"

Bella placed her finger gently on his mouth.

"We don't have all the answers right now," she said. "Luke, I've realized that no one ever has all the answers. But I've finally realized that I don't have to figure out everything on my own and neither do you. We have each other, and we have God."

"We have each other," Luke echoed, while he thanked God with his whole heart.

No matter what the challenges were on the road ahead, he trusted that the love he shared with Bella and the faith they shared in their Heavenly Father would see them through.

Epilogue

The following autumn

"I like the tiara on you," Luke said, then felt his grin widening. "Words I'm sure you thought you'd never hear from this rancher or any other."

His bride-to-be turned to him, the sparkle in her blue eyes overshadowed that of the tiara that adorned her fair hair.

"You don't think it's too much?"

"No, it's perfect for a city girl on the ranch."

Bella's smile told him she knew he was teasing.

The wedding shop's proprietor watched them with interest.

"I have to say," she remarked, "that I don't often see the groom take such an interest."

Luke carefully lifted the tiara off of Bella's head and handed it to the woman.

He put an arm around Bella's waist and said, "I guess we're just the kind of couple who likes to figure things out together."

It had indeed been a year of figuring things out together. Some fell into place in ways that clearly showed God's hand all over them, such as Lily and Alison being placed in a split grade seven and eight classroom so they could be a support to one another and the generous donations of time and financial support from the town to help get New Hope Ranch back on its feet again and start up the bed and breakfast that Bella had envisioned.

Others were still works in progress, like the legal action against Cal Wayman's fraud and Bella building up her resume as a ranching public relations expert, while also working at Jacob's café. She and Pastor Stewart were each other's biggest fans. People at the ranch were encouraged to check out the chapel nearby and those at church were told about the ranch.

She had started seeing a therapist about her past and had told her parents the truth about Lily's father. They expressed grief for her ordeal and regret that she hadn't felt she could come to them sooner.

Day by day, they were learning together to see God's hand in all things, even while they were still waiting for answers.

But, as they were discovering together, it was much easier to trust the waiting time and to trust how things would unfold when there was someone to share the journey with.

Each day it seemed they learned something new about each other. Bella also helped him understand himself better—he was slowly but surely easing himself out from the remembered weight of his late father's expectations of the kind of man he should be—and Luke prayed each day that he could be the man who would always ease Bella through any of her hurts, past, present or future.

They also learned to laugh together, there was so much joy and discovery as they prepared for the challenges of co-parenting, drummed up an increasing amount of PR work for Bella with the nearby businesses, and, together, worked to make the ranch not only a successful business but a home and haven for the years to come.

And now there was a wedding to plan, and that was another joy they could share together.

* * * * *

Dear Reader,

I often think about how there are two sides to being a writer. There's the part where we are mostly working alone. Then there's the part where we send our books out into the world.

This is the part that makes me so grateful to write for Love Inspired, because I believe we have the best readers any author could want.

The hero and heroine in this book both have things in their past that they wish they could change. With God's help, they learn to let go and move forward together.

If there are things in your past you are hanging on to, I pray that you will find the strength to let them go and trust in the happy future God has planned for you.

I would love to hear from you at deelynn1000@hotmail.com or you can find my author updates on Facebook.

Thank you.
Love,
Donna

Harlequin® Reader Service

Enjoyed your book?

Try the perfect subscription for Romance readers and get more great books like this delivered right to your door.

See why over 10+ million readers have tried Harlequin Reader Service.

Start with a Free Welcome Collection with free books and a gift—valued over $20.

Choose any series in print or ebook. See website for details and order today:

TryReaderService.com/subscriptions